Part One - The Beginning

Chapter 1

It was early enough in the morning that the dark sky had not yet welcomed the sunrise. Everything was silent; there were no trees rustling in the wind, no cars humming down the road, and no airplanes blasting through the frigid air.

A young man sat in his car in the parking lot of an airport. He was alone and scared, yet he wanted it no other way. This was something he had to do by himself. When the time came for him to enter the airport and prepare for his flight, he stepped out of his car, grabbed his luggage, and proceeded to the entrance of the building. After going through security scrutiny, the man sat down to begin the hour and a half wait for his flight. He had no interest in visiting any gift shops or restaurants in the airport. Instead, he pulled out his laptop, made a few clicks, then began typing.

Exactly three months into my sophomore year of high school I proclaimed my love for Summer Harris. I had been denying it for a long time to prevent a broken heart, but for some odd reason, this day changed everything. I was only a tenth grader in a school full of hundreds of upperclassmen, so it wasn't a huge proclamation where I stood on a lunch table and called out her name, expressing my never-ending love for her. Instead, it was me just telling my best friend, Shane, at our lunch table about the crush I had on this smoking hot senior.

"Nice, bro," Shane took a bite of his turkey sandwich. "She's a ten, but you'd never have a chance with her."

I laughed and played it off like I already knew I had no shot with her, but deep down the tiny possibility of her even talking to me was always in the back of my mind.

I pictured it like this: It would be another normal day of high school, and I would suddenly notice a group of guys catcalling a girl on my walk home. Being the "hero" I am, I would walk over to the group of guys only to realize they had been yelling offensive statements at Summer. I would then tell them to leave her alone (Of course, I know they would never take directions from a sophomore, but this is my fantasy!) and Summer would realize how lucky she was that I had been there to save the day. The rest would be history.

You can imagine every single scenario and replay it over and over again in your mind, but the reality is that is probably isn't going to happen the way you expect it to. You can't force something if it's already in the process of happening. I wish I would have known that then. It would have saved me a lot of time, stress, and sadness.

I still remember the exact date that I first told Shane I had a crush on Summer Harris. It was December 4, 2018. I remember it so clearly because December 4 was also the day I received an opportunity that would change my life. The opportunity itself didn't change my life, but rather the events that would lead up to it.

I was reading *Hamlet* in Mr. Glavier's fourth-hour English class right before lunch (where I would tell Shane about my love for Summer) when the class telephone rang.

"Okay, I'll tell him," Mr. Glavier hung up the phone and told me that my track coach wanted to see me.

I put down my copy of *Hamlet* and slowly took off for Coach Brothers' office two stories down. As much as I hated any kind of Shakespearean writing, I would have rather stayed in my English class than go see my coach to talk about running.

I was a state champion track runner my freshman year. I had broken six state records last year, including two of my own father's records. While it was safe to say I was a great runner, you couldn't say that I enjoyed it. Running for me is like reading; I only like doing it when I'm not being forced.

When my dad was in high school, he broke eighteen records and won the state championship all four years of his high school career. He was determined to be an Olympic runner for Team USA. He hadn't thought about a future that didn't involve track because he was so sure it was his destiny. But when he got to college, he hit a brick wall. As it turns out, he was only a decent competitor at the collegiate level. Perhaps he could have worked really hard and made the Olympics one day, but that was all thwarted when he broke his right foot in a bad fall his sophomore year. He wasn't able to run again until midway through his junior year, so he gave up his track dreams, threw away his running shoes, and started to focus on a new career. I won't bore you with all the big names and whatnot, but he pretty much works for a company that ruins people's lives by suing them.

Since he couldn't achieve what he had wanted so badly, the burden fell on the shoulders of his one and only child. At first I had liked running, but I quickly developed a dislike for the sport after being forced to train and compete tirelessly.

Anyway, I started walking to the stairs but took a quick detour, taking a left and starting for the stairs on the other side of the English wing. I did this for two reasons. One, I wanted to stay out of my English class as long as possible, and more importantly, I would pass Summer's second-hour class. As I got closer and closer to passing her classroom, I began checking my appearance in the camera of my phone, smoothing my hair down, making sure my hoodie was looking fresh, and wiping the corners of my mouth, even though I knew it was stupid because she probably wouldn't even see me.

I turned a corner and to my rare surprise, Summer was the first person I saw through the window. Her brown hair was flowing from a black hat that had a white puff at the top. She was laughing with her perfect set of teeth as her aqua-colored eyes looked at a picture someone was showing her. I kept making quick glances so she didn't catch me staring at her. I didn't want her getting the impression that I was a creep; it would have crushed me.

After what only felt like a split second, I walked on past the classroom and moved along to my coach's office. My chest and arms had developed a swoo feeling, while my heart was beating just like it was after I won the state race by .5637 seconds last year--a number that my dad had imprinted into my memory.

What is this feeling? Uriah, man, snap out of it. You can't be swooning over some girl!
I gave myself a mental pep talk.

It didn't work.

I had never been a sappy romantic, but right then and there, on December 4, 2017, I gave in and admitted I was in love with Summer Harris.

Chapter 2

My racing heartbeat didn't slow down until after I arrived at Coach Brothers' office. Then, nerves set in. I was dreading whatever was waiting for me behind the door that was plastered with athletic and health posters. My personal favorite (and by favorite I mean the most stupid one) was the large green poster that read, "Eat healthy! Run often! Sleep well! You are a teen! Do these three things, and you will be as strong as Mr. Green!" The poster featured a smiling, muscular piece of broccoli that was giving a thumbs up.

Before I knocked, I stopped and thought to myself, *what does he even do here?*

I mean, Coach Brothers was not really a teacher, just a track coach who had an office and always seemed to have plenty of free time. I still hadn't figured out what he did for the school besides constantly pester its best runner.

I raised my hand, knocked, and waited for a response. From experience I knew that Coach Brothers would either open up right away, as if he were standing by the door waiting for the knock, or he would leave you waiting, taking half a minute to get his butt up from his chair. It depended on if he wanted something from you or not.

The door opened before my hand even finished the second knock and I was greeted with a toothy smile.

"Uriah! How are you?" Coach Brothers asked.

"Hey, coach," I said taking a seat. "Pretty good, yourself?"

"Good...good," he said, closing the door behind him. "Are you excited for track season?"

"Of course," I lied.

"Well, then I have some good news for you!" he said while pulling out a stack of forms.

The mere sight of those forms made me cringe. It meant filling out a ton of paperwork, reading long liability sheets, and agreeing to the official rules and terms of another stupid track race. I should have known. Coach Brothers had called me down because he wanted me to race once again at another event.

"I'm sure you must know what this means by now?" he chuckled.

"I think so. Another race?"

"No."

My heart sprung up from the valley of dread. Maybe I wouldn't have to wake up at a ridiculous time after all. Maybe I wouldn't have to spend an entire day stuck with hundreds of other people who actually liked the sport. Maybe I wouldn't have to face the constant pressure I my father released on me every single time I had a race.

"Wait, what?" I leaned forward in my seat.

"Haha, I'm just messing with you! Most definitely another race! Ann Arbor!"

Of course.

"Now, the race is still a month away, but I wanted you to give Rich all the paperwork for him to fill out and then we can together and start taking a look at all the other runners. There will be some pretty decent kids there, but I think you will do well."

He handed me the first sheet of paper, which explained the details of the race. The next paper was a sign-up form that my coach would send back to Ann Arbor. The rest was a bunch of medical liability forms that my dad would have to sign.

"So, you take this and sign here," he handed me the sign-up sheet. "And, you take these home, get them signed, and bring them back as soon as possible."

Coach Brothers and my father had basically forced me to compete in three races since my freshman year ended. The first one was in Indianapolis, where the top 500 runners in the nation competed. For my particular event, there were 126 runners who were all ranked based off of time. Once all of the races came to an end, it was revealed to us that I had placed ninth.

My dad didn't talk to me the entire ride home.

The other two races were both in Detroit and were a lot smaller events. I finished both in first place and my dad was so excited that I was able to convince him to stop at a nice restaurant and have a quality meal for once. Not to sound cocky, but it was normal for me to win races. What made those two wins so special was that I beat out one of the fastest high schoolers in the country by only a few hundredths of a second.

The news of another race made me want to retreat into solitude, so I filled out what I needed to and got out of Coach Brothers' office as quickly as possible. My whole day--no, my whole month--had been ruined. I would spend the holidays dreading the race and being pestered by my father to train during every free moment.

Of course, it would all be different if I had a purpose to run, you know? A reason to be motivated. Some nights before bed I would fantasize about a scenario where Summer was sitting in the stands cheering me on as I blew out the competition. If running would impress Summer, maybe I would actually want to run. But she would never come watch a track race, let alone come to watch the scrawny sophomore who no one paid any attention to.

Although another race was the last thing I wanted to do, I tried to find the positives in the situation. At least it was in the hometown of my favorite college team. Maybe my dad would let me see "the Big House," the Michigan Wolverines football stadium.

If he even goes.

The University of Michigan was where his track dreams fell apart. The heartbreak might be too much for him to want to return. Maybe I'll be able to go alone.

Chapter 3

My mother died when I was just a year old. I would say she passed away but it's really hard to soften the way that she left this Earth. Speculation and heartache is all we have from that night. My dad was on a business trip in California and since I was only an infant, there were no witnesses and the murderer got away.

The police believed, from what they found, that someone had jumped at an opportunity to make some extra cash when they saw that our living room window was open. Whoever it was broke through the screen and began stealing my parents' most valuable possessions. A crash must have startled my mom from her sleep and headed downstairs to see what was going on. When my babysitter arrived the next morning, she found my mother dead on the stairway. My mom's flower vase was laying in the dining room floor, shattered in a million pieces. Mom had been shot three times.

Luckily for me, the intruder hadn't known I was in the house and fled right after they murdered my mom.

When I was little, my father only told me this story in few details, but one thing I will never forget is him talking about how it almost killed him, literally. He became so depressed afterward that he refused to do anything but lie in bed. About five months after my mom died, my dad was going to attempt suicide by jumping off a bridge, but law enforcement convinced him to step down.

Quite something to hear from your father when you ask where mommy is, isn't it?

I'm told my dad was actually a decent human being before my mom died. My parents met in college after my dad broke his foot. They fell in love quickly and married two years later. As a child, I spent many weekends at my grandparents' house and they always told me stories of how happy my parents were together. Mom apparently made him a better person. I cling to the thought that if she were still alive we would be a happy, normal family. Especially on nights like December 4, 2017.

"Hey," I closed the front door.

My dad was in his office typing something on his laptop. I barely even got a grunt out of him.

I ran up my stairs, the same ones my mom had walked down to meet her untimely death, and threw my backpack on my bed. I would deal with my homework later. Right now I had to try and get out of this race. I could, of course, just not tell my dad about it, but I'd already tried that once before and it hadn't work. My coach would just end up calling my dad and I would be in bigger trouble for not telling him.

I ran back down the stairs, taking two at a time, with the papers in my hands.

"Hey, dad, I have to show you something," I said walking into his office.

"Yeah?" he said without looking at me.

"'Another race," I said holding up the papers.

Suddenly what seemed so important on his computer didn't matter anymore.

"Really? Let me see!" he exclaimed excitedly with a huge smile on his face.

I gave him the papers and he began to look through them. As I observed his facial expressions, I knew he had just seen that it was in Ann Arbor.

"Yeah, you don't have to come if you don't want," I told him. "I mean, I am not sure if I even wanna go."

"I'll think about it. But you, you are definitely going. This is a great opportunity, boy."

"No, I don't want to. I've already done three, and I really do not want to train all Christmas break!" I protested.

"Why not?" he asked as he stood up. "What else have you got to do? It's not like you have any friends."

"How would you know?" I rolled my eyes at him. "'Cause you are just the best dad in the world?"

"Uriah, I want you to be great!" he shouted back, throwing a pen on the floor.

"Dad, you know I am already a crazy fast runner!" I paused. "But you don't understand it. I hate running."

My dad took three steps toward me and slapped me forcefully across the face, sending a stinging sensation throughout my jaw.

"You are going to that race, and I don't care how much you don't like it. You are going to train and you are going to win. Go to your room, do your homework, then go for a run. I want at least three miles tonight. You can find yourself dinner. I'm very busy with work."

And with that, he slammed the door on me as I stood there rubbing my numb face.

Chapter 4

The sting from the slap remained all night even after the pain and redness went away. It wasn't exactly surprising for him to hit me, but he hadn't done it in a very long time. It didn't matter if he struck my face every day or once a year, one time was way too many.

I hated him.

I pulled out my English homework and a pencil. I had to write at least twenty-five lines about something I loved. The first thought that came to my mind was Summer. Besides my mom, she was the only other person who just the mere thought of comforted me. The only problem with that was Summer didn't even know my name.

The first word I wrote was the word Summer, but then I paused.

Should I write about her? I asked myself.

No, too risky. Too embarrassing.

I flipped my pencil over to erase her name, but the eraser on my pencil had been completely diminished. I could've scratched her name out but I was too OCD to do that. Oh well, I could just write about the season.

I then proceeded to write about summer, not Summer. I wrote about how much I loved the beach and how beautiful it was, every part of it. From the feet-burning sand to the breaktaking views. The way the water feels after a long sweaty run. The way I feel during every single sunset. Nothing beats sunsets in Michigan. The sky is filled with red, orange, yellow, and every color in between. It is like God has a pallet of every single shade on the color wheel and each night he picks different colors to splatter across his sky canvas.

After I explained why I loved the beach and summer, in incredibly wordy details so I could stretch it out to twenty-five lines, I moved on to my math homework. The homework was pretty simple that night, just problems twenty problems of solving algebraic equations. When I finished that, I was done for the night.

I zipped up my backpack and threw it by my desk where it would be left untouched until tomorrow morning. I changed into my running clothes--an Adidas sweatshirt, Nike leggings, and Nike shorts--and put on my white Mizuno shoes and headed for the kitchen. I couldn't leave without my traditional ham and cheese sandwich pre-run meal. I slowly made and ate the sandwich, dreading the three-mile long run that awaited me. It was not physically challenging for me, but it took away time that I could be using to read Harry Potter or play Madden.

Once I took the last bite of my sandwich, I made my way to my driveway. My father was still behind his closed door, working on who knows what. Probably ruining someone else's life.

I stepped outside, turned on some Lil Yachty, and started my stretches. My body shivered in the December air, but I knew it would warm up eventually. After loosening up my joints, I took a left turn and heading off toward my destination. It was the same route I had taken for weeks now.

I steadied my breath every few seconds to help pace myself. I planned on running much farther than the 800-

meters I'd be running in Ann Arbor. Three-mile runs meant about six intervals of 800 meters. My goal was to get faster with every 800 meters. It was a long shot, even for me, but it was a good goal. The first 800, I ran at a pretty good pace. My phone buzzed and I stopped to look at my time.

Distance: 800 meters

Time: 2:14 minutes

Not bad for a first run. I then selected the button reading "New 800" and began to run again. I was getting closer and closer to my destination, only a little bit longer. After what felt like a very long time, there was another buzz. I dreaded looking at this one.

Distance: 800 meters

Time: 2:11 Minutes

Hmm. It was better than I had expected. I knew I needed to run with bigger strides during the next leg of my run. Motivating me more was my finish line, my halfway point. When the third buzz vibrated in my hand, I stopped and looked up from the ground. I knew where I had ended up but I wanted to check my time first.

Distance: 800 meters

Time: 2:04 Minutes

I smiled. That was a huge improvement. I looked up, and sure enough, just like I had planned it, there was Summer's house. I stood on the other side of the street pretending to check my pulse so not to seem creepy. A couple of months earlier, I had learned that Summer lived really close to me and I changed my running route so it would take me right by her house.

I kept glancing up at the white, two-story house, trying to catch glimpses of any activity, when something different caught my eye. A car was parked on the side of the street next to their house.

Must be a relative, I thought.

That idea quickly faded when I saw an upstairs' light flicker on. I caught a glimpse of a large, muscular man. Having to squint to focus, I realized it was the jock of my high school, Davy Trick.

Davy, the quarterback of the football team, was one of the most popular guys in school. Yet, he only had one playoff win, while I had won state. Even though I was better at my sport than he was at his, he got all the attention. Apparently even Summer's, as she was now sitting next to him, laughing.

They were playing some kind of game but I didn't know what, nor did I want to know. It was just my luck to have my crush hanging out with the biggest prick in our high school. He had never done me wrong personally, but because Shane was on the football team, I had heard some stories.

Shane moved here from Indiana and on the first day of football, Davy asked him to meet him behind the school. Shane, not wanting to be both the new guy and the team loser, did as he was asked and was jumped by Davy and his friends. Shane broke one of their noses and gave the other a black eye. He kicked Davy right in the balls, too. Unfortunately, Shane got the worst of the fight. His whole body was covered in bruises and the punches they threw at him were so brutal that it caused him to puke. All because he had shown interest in the quarterback position.

Every time I heard or saw the praise Davy received, I wanted to yell out that he was a jerk who jumped people for no good reason. But, I was too scared to say or do anything. Shane, on the other hand, called him Davy Prick.

I put my headphones back in and headed back home. I was too upset to run slow. I finished my last three races with the times of *2:04, 2:03, and 2:01*.

Chapter 5

The next morning I woke up to the signed race forms laying outside my bedroom door. Dad must have already left for a meeting or something.

I walked downstairs and went through my normal school morning routine, which included making banana toast and sometimes playing a quick game on Madden. I walked to school every single day. My dad was too selfish to take me on the days he was home, but I had too much pride to ride the bus, and I didn't have my license yet. Fortunately, my school was only a half mile away. Unfortunately, it was single-digit weather.

With every few steps I took, I was greeted with my icy, visible breath. The closer I got to my school, the lighter the sky became. When I finally stepped foot on the school grounds, I heard the passing time bell ring so I started walking a little faster. After I was inside the building, my mind subconsciously started looking around for Summer, but I didn't see her. The clock hit 7:59 a.m. and I hurried to my first-hour history class. I turned the corner and fist-bumped Mr. Lamper, who was holding the door open for everyone.

That hour we were working on a project about the nuclear bombings of Hiroshima and Nagasaki to finish up our World War II unit. But instead of actually working on our project, Shane and I talked in a work room.

"No way!" his jaw dropped.

"Yep."

"Davy Prick?"

"Yes."

"With Summer?"

"Yes, dude. I told you."

Shane was a bit of a drama queen. He loved some good gossip.

"I hate that guy! That sucks. Sorry, bro," Shane said as he opened up his school laptop.

"Yeah, I mean, he's never done anything to me but..." I started before being cut off.

"Um, yeah he has. He beat me up. Your best friend! That's almost like beating you up too," Shane flipped his shaggy, dirty blonde hair out of his face. I had pretty wavy hair, but I could never deal with hair like his that always fell right above the eyes. But Shane seemed to embrace it when he was getting fired up.

"Yeah, I guess," I said. "She could do so much better."

"Who? You?" he mocked me.

"Shut up!" I laughed at his sarcasm and threw a pen at him.

"Seriously, bro, just give it up," Shane threw the pen back at me.

I didn't respond, but instead picked up the pen and chucked it really hard at him. Game on. I threw the pen sidearm and it nailed him on the side of his arm, causing him to fake-howl in pain. He recovered, picked the pen back up, and threw it toward me like a knife, but it was slow enough for me to catch. I was just about to throw it again when there was a knock on the door.

I paused.

The worried look on Shane's face suggested to me that it might have been the last person I wanted to see at that very moment--Summer. Hundreds of people in our high school, and it had to be Summer Harris knocking on the door. But, why?

Oh, crap. Crap. Crap. Crap, I thought. *How idiotic did I look playing pen war with my friend?*

This was the official end of my chances, though they were very slim to begin with.

I slowly swiveled my chair around and to my relief, it was Mr. Lamper. The fact I had been relieved to see a teacher instead of Summer said a lot about how much I liked this girl.

When the bell rang signaling the end of first hour, Shane and I continued our conversation.

"Okay, but listen to this, bro," Shane walked alongside me. "I might have scored this babe. We are going to lunch today."

On the inside, I was disappointed. I would have to sit alone at lunch, something that made me feel like dying when

I had to do it. On the outside though, I appeared excited for Shane.

"Really? Who?"

"Camilla Ervancio," he smiled.

"Wait, the foreign exchange student?" I started laughing.

"Yeah, what's wrong with that?" Shane looked around to make sure no one was eavesdropping.

"Nothing. I mean, she's attractive and all, but she only knows like ten English words," I hushed my laugh.

"Well, yeah," he turned red. "But she understood what I meant when I asked her out."

We walked up to Coach Brothers' office and I began pulling out the papers for the race. Shane looked at me in disgust and said, "Another race?"

I'd completely forgotten to tell Shane about the race amidst all of the Summer and Davy shock, but we were too close to Coach Brothers' office for me to say too much. I nodded as I looked for the last paper in the bottom of my backpack.

"Yeah, Ann Arbor. My dad is making me. We got in fight."

I decided to leave out the part where he slapped me. Partly because I didn't want my dad to get in trouble, but mostly because I was embarrassed. I had never told anyone about the abuse I received from my dad, and I didn't plan on telling a single soul anytime soon.

"Sucks for you. Hey, you know what? I'm gonna see if Coach Brothers has any races that I could do," Shane said. He was on the track team too, but he was pretty slow so football suited him better.

"Why would you waste your time if you don't have to?" I knocked on the door.

It took a while for coach to open the door, but once he finally did, the last part of his donut was being stuffed into his mouth.

"Uriah! Thank you!" he took the papers and looked them over. "You are all set. Come by my office tomorrow and we'll start looking at the other runners."

Coach Brothers turned to go back into his office, but Shane stopped him.

"Coach, do you have any events for a 200-meter run?"

"I'm sorry, I don't believe we've met! New runner?" Coach Brothers reached out and shook Shane's hand.

"Um," Shane looked over at me, confused. "I am on the track team, coach. Shane..."

"Wow! Shane, you've grown! Your hair is so long now that I didn't even recognize you!" Coach Brothers laughed.

Shane chuckled and played along with Coach Brothers' excuse for not knowing who he was.

"But sadly, no, I do not have anything for you! Well, get to class now, boys!"

Shane and I followed his instructions and took off our separate ways for class, but before he rounded the corner I heard him mutter, "My hair has always been this long."

Chapter 6

Nothing significant happened until later that night when two things combined to put me into a very bad mood. The first came right after I finished up my English homework: writing at least twenty-five lines of something that you hate. I zipped up my backpack and threw it into my designated "backpack spot" to the left of my desk. Grabbing my phone off my nightstand, I started scrolling through Instagram. The first picture I came across was of a girl in her "adorable" winter apparel, holding a coffee. Typical. The second picture was a junior from my school posing with his friend in their basketball uniforms while making a "W" with their fingers. I quickly scrolled by the first two pictures but a third photo stopped me dead in my tracks. I recognized the profile picture and Instagram tag: *SummerHarr1s*

My heart fluttered just like it did every time I saw Summer had new posts. It either meant a sexy selfie or a small glimpse into her life, the one that I so desperately longed to be a part of. This time when the picture loaded, however, the pounding stopped in my chest. Instead, it thumped up painfully into my neck. There she was, the love of my life, with her arms wrapped around Davy's neck, a huge childlike smile on her face. He was laughing, entranced with her presence.

In immediate jealousy, I declared my hatred for, as Shane called him, Davy Prick.

How lucky, I thought. *Why him?*

I scrolled down just a little farther to read the caption. It read: *This one* <3 <3 <3

How sappy. I hated those heart emojis. I hated this post. Mostly because, in my eyes, I should've been the one she was hanging all over.

I took a screenshot of the picture and sent it to Shane. This would end up being the second thing that put me in a bad mood.

Shane replied ten minutes later.

Shane: So, it's confirmed. Rest in peace, buddy…

Me: Ha. Ha. Definition of a night ruiner.

Shane: It won't last lol. He's going to some college in Ohio for football.

Me: Yeah, but then what? She's going to college too.

Shane: Oh, shoot, yeah. I think she Tweeted once about NC State.

Me: Where's that?

Shane: North Carolina. Just give it up.

I knew I had to take Shane's advice and, indeed, give it up, but that is easier said than done. At this point in my life I had come to one conclusion: all the fairytales you hear about with perfect, happy endings are just not reality. Only a select amount of people in this world get a miracle. The rest of us just have to listen to them tell their story over and over again and hope that maybe one day we too will receive our very own miracle.

Shane sent another message two minutes later.

Shane: But dude... lunch today with Camilla was amazing.

Me: Yeah? How'd it go?

Shane: I'll just say this... she didn't need to know any English for us to have fun.

Me: Lol omg… so we still on for Wendy's tomorrow?

Shane took about a half an hour to respond.

Shane: Nah, I can't. Sorry. I'm going out with Camilla again.

Me: Wow, okay.

Shane: But, hey! When you and Summer get together ;) we can double date.

I didn't respond. I was hoping he wouldn't be this type of friend. You know, the type that completely ditches you once they get a girlfriend.

You're over exaggerating, I thought. *It was one time!*

But then I started thinking about what I would do at lunch tomorrow. Sitting alone at lunch just wouldn't do. I would never be able to get with a girl like Summer if I was that much of a loser.

Stop, I told myself. *Give it up already.*

I was never going to end up with her. It would save me a lot of time and stress if I just accepted that fact now.

I put my phone back on my nightstand and grabbed a sweatshirt. I bolted down my stairs and out my front door, stopping at the end of my driveway. I hurried through my stretches; I needed to run. Because I had done it so many times before, I subconsciously took off toward Summer's house, but when I realized what I was doing, I altered my route.

I didn't care about distances or times, I just ran. The way running is supposed to be. Pretty soon I regretted wearing a sweatshirt because I was burning up. I was running faster and longer than I ever had; I'm pretty sure if I was timing myself I would have broken my personal record. But that did not matter right now. What mattered was getting all this anger and sadness out of my system. If running for me was just like this, I am pretty sure I would still love it. I had never felt more energized physically, yet this feeling of sadness still loomed over my whole presence. With every step and breath in the cold winter air, every bad aspect of my life flashed before my eyes. I saw Shane not even looking at me in the hallways. I saw my dad slapping me across the face. I saw myself running in a track race. Worst of all, I saw Summer and her not knowing who I am.

I was so lost in my thoughts, having a pity party, that I forgot it was December in Michigan. I hadn't been paying attention to the slippery streets like I normally did.

Too late now.

Everything suddenly felt in slow motion. My body slid and I found myself flying toward the cold, slippery ground. I felt a burning sensation from the top of my left eyebrow all the way down to my lower lip. Then, everything went black.

When I regained consciousness, I didn't know where I was or what time it was. There was nobody around and all the houses nearby seemed to be lifeless. I was so cold that the numbness took away all the pain until I touched a finger to my face. It burned and ached at the same time. Involuntarily, I pulled my hand away to find my shaking hand covered in blood. Looking over on the ground, I saw a few splatters of my blood near where I hit the ice. To top it all off, my practically brand new, white Nike sweatshirt was completely ruined.

I stood up and tried taking a few steps, but I felt woozy. I needed to try to get home. It was way too cold and my face was way too messed up for me to stay out any longer. I kept trudging on through the black and white spots in my vision before I couldn't stand it anymore and sat back down on a curb.

I decided to call Shane and have him come pick me up. I reached for my phone in my right pocket, but it wasn't there. I patted my left pocket. Not there either. I tried to remember if I had forgotten it where I had the accident, but then the terrible thought flowed back to me: I left my phone at home.

I didn't know what I was going to do. I weighed every possible option, but in my condition, none of them were possible. I had to do something, though. My body was getting colder with every second and the pain was now excruciating.

I sat back down on the curb with my head in my hands. Perhaps I could go and start knocking on doors, but who would really answer a knock on their door at nine at night?

Just when I was about to give up all hope, I felt something warm and furry brush up against me. I turned to find a golden retriever, who was acting like I was his owner and I'd been gone for the entire day. I started petting the dog and giving it affection back while I looking around for its owner. There was no one. I tried looking at the dog's tag, but my hands were shaking way too much. Just as the dog was trying to lick my bloody face, I heard, "MARVIN? COME HERE BOY!"

There was a man bundled up in winter gear running my way carrying a broken leash. He had beady eyes that were strangely welcoming. He was wearing a black winter hat, but his gray hair stuck out from underneath it at the top of his large forehead. I prayed he would have a phone or that he lived nearby.

"Hey, sorry about that pal! This leash has been really old for a long time," he gestured to a broken leash. "Ought to get a new one! Thanks... what in the world happened to you?"

I stared at the man, wondering if I should protect myself from embarrassment, but his welcoming eyes told me otherwise. "I was running and, uh, fell. I blacked out and I don't have a phone. Do you have one I can borrow?" I pleaded.

"Oh my, of course, pal! I am so sorry! Here!" he handed me his phone quickly with the dial pad already up. "Better call one of your parents."

"Thank you," my teeth chattered as I typed in Shane's number. My dad was probably passed out drunk on the couch by now.

The phone rang four times before Shane answered with uncertainty at the unknown number, "Hello...?"

"Shane. Hey this is Uri. Um, I need you to do me a big, huge favor."

"Depends."

"No, I'm serious. I had a bad accident and I need to get home ASAP."

"Dang. Whose phone?" Shane asked, obviously thinking that I was exaggerating.

"This guy walking his dog. Listen, I really need you to come pick me up. I slipped and fell. My face is all bloody, and I feel dizzy when I stand."

The man looked at me with concern like I was his very own son. Honestly, he had acted more like a father to me in his two minutes of knowing me than my dad had in the past five years.

"Oh crap, seriously? Okay, where are you? I'm on my way," Shane said, finally realizing the severity of my phone call.

I pulled the phone away from my throbbing face and asked the man, "Um, where are we?"

"Corner of 5th and Comber Street," the man recited to me after looking at the nearest road signs.

I repeated the streets to Shane, and he said, "Okay, hang in there, buddy. I'll be there as soon as possible."

I hung up the call and gave the man his phone back.

Maybe Shane wasn't a bad friend after all. Maybe I was just overreacting.

Chapter 7

"If you don't mind me asking, why were you out running this late at night?" the man questioned. We still hadn't exchanged names.

"Um," I started running my hand through my hair like I always did when I was nervous. "I wasn't having a good night, so I decided to go on a run. I hit an icy spot and then blacked out."

"Ah, a good run always eases the mind. Ice can be very dangerous this time of the year."

"How bad is it?" I felt the stinging along the entire right side of my face.

"Pretty bad, kid. I would go home and have your mom check that out!"

"Yeah. Definitely," I shied off at the end and started kicking a chunk of ice on the ground. I didn't feel like telling him that my mom was dead and sharing the whole story. It sucked having to retell a story like that over and over again. I could tell he sensed something sensitive with the topic. He had just started to say something when I heard the loud, broken muffler of Shane's car.

"That must be him," I said, looking around for headlights, thankful to get out of that awkward situation.

Sure enough, Shane's car came speeding around a corner down the street. The man and I stared at the car simultaneously as it quickly approached us. As it got closer and closer, I began to see more details of the car, the front license plate, the Toyota symbol on the front bumper, and then worst of all, the shadow of a girl in the front seat.

Camilla.

The car stopped right next to us and Camilla looked petrified when she saw me.

Was it really that bad? I wondered.

Leave it to Shane to come to my rescue and drag along his foreign exchange student girlfriend, who I didn't even know.

Shane rolled down Camilla's window.

"Hey, man, let's get you home!"

"Yeah," I walked toward Shane's car then turned back to the man. "Thank you, sir. I don't know what I would've done without you!"

"Don't mention it, kid. Take it easy!" he waved and started walking away with his dog.

Instant awkwardness filled the car as soon as I took a seat. Shane stared at my face in awe, but Camilla acted like she would catch a disease if she even acknowledged me.

"That is sick, dude. You'll have a crazy looking scar that's for sure. Here let me take a picture!" Shane pulled out his phone.

"No, stop," I protested.

"Here, look."

"No."

"Dude, come on..."

"I SAID NO!" I yelled. I shocked myself by yelling like that, and Shane was staring at me like I had no skin. I had never yelled at him, not in that way. I thought it had been weird before, but you could almost now feel the tension in the air now.

After what seemed like forever, Shane finally said, "Uriah, this is my girlfriend, Camilla."

Unbelievable. They were dating now? As far as I knew, tonight was only their second time ever hanging out. The way he introduced me to her was like I was some stranger they were meeting for the first time. It was terrible.

"Hi," she spoke quietly. All she said was the one word, but you could definitely tell she had a strong Colombian accent.

I built up all the strength I could to be nice to this girl. Iit wasn't her fault and I was seeing a lot of my dad in myself these past few minutes; I was not going to act like he did.

"Hi, Camilla," I half smiled back.

The rest of the car ride was silent. It was a relief to see my two-story craftsman home. I said a quick 'thank you' to Shane and got out of the car. He felt like a stranger to me now. In a matter of twelve hours, our friendship had taken a drastic turn.

Before I even got into the house, Shane's car was out of sight, but I could still hear it. I put my hand on the chilled door knob and twisted it to the right. As soon as I entered the house a wave of warmth hit me, which felt so good on my face.

I had only taken one step into my living room before the stench of alcohol hit my nose. Maybe it was from the fall, or maybe it was from the smell, but I suddenly felt like I was going to puke. My dad was passed out on the couch with a beer bottle still in his hand. On the floor next to him was about half a dozen more empty bottles.

I don't know if my dad drank like this before my mom died, but I'm assuming he didn't. He didn't necessarily drink every day, but I think when the thought of my mom hit him hard, so did the alcohol. Whenever he drank, he either passed out or became extremely drunk. And when he was drunk, he had two moods--emotional or angry--and they were both equally atrocious.

When he was emotionally drunk, my father would often cry and reveal to me things he otherwise never talked about. One night when I was eleven, he told me all about his first date with mom and how he had brought her a lily. They went to a fancy restaurant that his parents had given him money for and afterwards, they walked the streets of the town talking about life. That night was one of my favorites ever. Even though I spent it alone after my dad finally passed out, I clung to the hope that everything would be better from then on. My dad had finally talked to me about something other than running, and it was amazing.

The next morning, however, was a huge disappointment. I woke up and ran down the stairs to ask my dad more about mom, but once I started asking him questions, like where she had grown up and what was her favorite book, he had no memory of the previous night and was a completely different person..

"What? Uriah, go away, please. I'm busy," he never even looked at me, despite the night before when he couldn't break eye contact.

My dad's next kind of drunk was fueled by anger. I had learned to stay away from him when he was like this. Otherwise, almost every encounter with him ended up with a slap across my face or a bottle being thrown at me as I ran out of the room. When I played invisible when he was angry-drunk, I was abused a lot less. Sober slaps only occurred occasionally.

I can only thank God that my father was passed out when I walked into the house with a bloody face. I couldn't deal with anything else right now. I rushed upstairs and locked myself into the bathroom. I almost didn't recognize myself in the mirror. The entire right side of my face was cut and bruised. The line of the cut ran from the end of my eyebrow all the way down to my upper lip. I observed my face closely and found bits and pieces of gravel stuck in my frosty face. I pulled out a washcloth and ran it under warm water until it was completely soaked, slowly applied it to my face, endured the immediate pain, and then felt the relieving warmth against my skin.

Chapter 8

I didn't sleep very well that night. Apparently I switch positions a lot when I'm sleeping because I woke up multiple times with my face stinging from contact with my pillow. When I woke up to get ready for school, I found blood stains splattered across my pillow, prompting me to throw my dirty pillowcase down the laundry chute. I washed my face again and tried to make the gauze pad look presentable. After many failed attempts, I gave up. It would have to be fine.

When I walked downstairs, I didn't know how my dad would react. I hadn't had an injury this severe since I was a little kid. I turned into the kitchen and found him sitting at the kitchen table with coffee and his laptop.

"Hey," I said, knowing eventually I would have to tell him or he wouldn't even look up to notice at all.

"Hey, champ," he replied while taking a sip of his coffee. Normally a son would love to be called champ by their father, but my dad only says it to remind me that I can sink no lower than champion.

When I didn't respond, he added, "Did you run last night?"

"Yeah, and um, this happened," I said so he would finally look at me.

He winced, pulling back his jaw to reveal clenched teeth. I barely even recognized his hungover face anymore.

"Ouch. How'd you do that?" he acted as if it were just a bad paper cut.

"I was running and slipped and fell on the ice," I said as I turned and starting warming up some freezer waffles. I was a fool for thinking he would actually care.

"Geesh, well you'd better ice that," he said, turning back to his computer.

"Yep," I said quietly.

You would think he would take the hint that I was upset. Or, maybe he knew and just didn't care.

I spent my entire walk to school planning what I was going to say to Shane, who I hoped to confront in our first-hour class. He was going overboard with this whole Camilla thing. Yes, it had only been a couple times, but I needed him way more than she did. She probably didn't even understand most of the things he said!

Mr. Lamper finally let me into the classroom after a major interrogation about my face, and I tried ignoring all the whispers and stares from my classmates as I walked over to my seat beside Shane. By the time I had sat down, it was too quiet to confront him. Some brave girl finally broke the silence, "What happened to your face, Uriah?"

Every single eye in the classroom turned to me. It was awesome, yet terrifying. I loved the attention--the type I never got at home--but at the same time it was very awkward. I looked over to the girl and said, "I was running last night and I slipped and fell on the ice."

I should have tried to come up with a better story, but I couldn't think of anything impressive that quickly. A few people expressed their "ouch's" as Mr. Lamper started his discussion on communism.

I didn't pay attention to anything during that class period besides Shane. He didn't seem to be acting any differently, occasionally showing me a dirty drawing in his notes or whispering something in my ear. Typical Shane. As if he hadn't been choosing his new girlfriend over me or didn't notice that my face was completely jacked up.

After a page full of notes that I had no comprehension of taking, the bell rang throughout the school, signaling the end of first period. Shane and I packed our bags up and started walking in the same direction down the hallway. Now was the time. I had just started to say, "Hey, dude…" when my heart skipped a beat. Davy Trick was down the hall holding hands with Summer on one side and laughing with his friend, Cam, on the other.

Shane seemed to notice too, but he wasn't as intimidated as me, or at least he didn't seem to show it. I carefully observed Summer. She had such a blank expression on her pale and beautiful face that I couldn't tell if she was enjoying being with Davy or not.

As soon as Davy, Summer, and I crossed paths in the hallway, Davy stopped and patted his friend on the arm, both of them looking at my face like I had leprosy. Summer looked too. I could feel myself blushing as I stopped, frowning at Davy. I don't know where I got the confidence to give him a dirty look, but it was probably because I was trying to impress Summer or have her pity the fact that Davy was making fun of me.

"Ay, Cam, look at Shane's friend," they pointed and laughed at my face. "He looks like Shane after we were done with him."

The two started howling in laughter. I don't understand how any human being could laugh so hard at something that caused someone else so much discomfort and pain. I could feel myself getting red now. I was being humiliated in front of the girl I loved. Yes, I loved her. I wasn't going to hide from it anymore; it just made everything worse. It had been so excruciating ignoring what had been spinning in my head for weeks now.

I looked at Summer first. She was gently tapping Davy on the hand she had been holding and mouthing the word "stop." It was comforting because she now knew I existed and she had the decency to stick up for me, yet it was embarrassing due to the circumstances. The only encounter she had with me was because I was the nameless, skinny sophomore that her boyfriend was making fun of.

It wasn't necessarily ideal.

"Oh, really?" Shane set his backpack down on the ground and walked toward them. I wish I had the guts or nerve to walk that close. I wasn't necessarily scared to walk by Davy, but I was scared to walk by Summer.

"Yeah, buddy," Davy treated Shane as if he were a kid, patting him on the shoulder.

"Hmm, no, I think you got it wrong. You had to have THREE people to jump me. If you were really brave, I think you would have taken me one on one," Shane said as he pushed away Davy's arm.

"You wanna go at it again? One on one? Maybe we can have that ugly exchange student watch? Show her what a real man looks like," Davy pounded his fist, causing Summer to rub her temple in distress. Amidst the rising tensions between Shane and Davy, I couldn't help but think, *Gosh she's hot.*

"Davy, just... stop. Okay?" she pleaded with him.

At this point, I was completely out of the picture. It had all started with me, but now this was between Davy and Shane. Summer looked over at me as Shane and Davy kept exchanging threats. I wondered what Summer would think if she knew that the sophomore she was looking at has the biggest crust on her. Would she think it was creepy? Would she think it was sweet? Or, maybe even a little of both?

"What was it then?" the argument recaptured my attention. "Scared I was going to take your precious little quarterback position?"

"You have a lot of confidence for a sophomore," Davy got closer to Shane's face. I could sense a fight about to happen.

Just as Davy was about to shove Shane, a small, Asian teacher came running from her classroom and set them straight. She sent Davy, Summer, and Cam in one direction, and Shane and me in another.

"Come on," he pulled my shoulder as we started walking the opposite direction, hearing the laughs of Davy and his friend mocking my face again.

"Ignore them, Uriah," he said when he caught me looking back. Summer had her head turned over her shoulder and was looking right at me. Our eyes connected and it was like I could read her thoughts. She was saying, "Sorry about that."

I turned my head back around with contentment. All of what happened suddenly didn't seem too bad anymore. In a way, I felt like she had sided with me. In the total opposite way, she was too scared or too embarrassed to actually stick up for me. Nevertheless, this small encounter sent a spark through my entire body. I felt like maybe this was a start.

But there was one huge problem with this theory: Summer had walked away with Davy, not with me.

Chapter 9

I decided to put my confrontation with Shane on hold until he started ditching me for Camilla again. After all, he had completely stuck up for me and not let Davy embarrass me any further. I don't know what the heck I would have done had he not been there, so I definitely owe him one.

I spent the rest of the day thinking about Summer and how close of an encounter we had. If only I would have braved up and said something. I don't know what I would have said, but it's easy to think of all sorts of comebacks after the encounter is over with.

Constant stares from classmates, teachers, and even custodians couldn't even distract me from thoughts of Summer.

What if she isn't the person I think she is? I asked myself. It's hard to love someone and then learn about their hamartia. You just want them to be perfect and when you learn that they aren't, you try to deny it. *Was Summer's flaw that she was attracted to guys like Davy? Is she as mean as*

Davy? Is she a mean girl? Hundreds of thoughts raced through my mind. With every negative thought about Summer though, came a counterclaim to remind me that she was indeed a good person.

I was finally able to free my mind a little bit when I went into Coach Brothers' office for a meeting about my track race that was a few weeks away. When I walked into his office, he rushed over to me like an emergency room doctor.

"Uriah! What in the heck happened?" he said, pulling a chair over for me to sit down.

"I was running last night, and I slipped and fell on the ice," I retold the story for what seemed like the thousandth time.

"Really? Are you okay?" he asked me. I had never seen my coach this worried.

"Yeah," I shrugged. "It hurts, but I'll be fine."

"Well, that's certainly great, but I mean… are you okay to run? Did you mess up your technique?"

This guy literally had no freaking sensor.

My face was completely screwed up and he still cared more about my running ability. I was nothing more to him than a body that could run fast and bring glory to my school's track program.

"Um, yes," I snarkily replied. "I think I had just better not run for a little while."

"Well, I suppose you can do that. If your father agrees, of course. I don't really see how your face affects your legs though…"

He was trying to guilt me. It wouldn't work though. I had already made up my mind that I was not running for, at least, a few days.

"I'm feeling confident with my running," I remarked. "Before I fell, I was running at an all-time high."

"Were you really? Times?" he chuckled in happiness.

"Just under a minute and fifty-nine seconds," I lied. This number would make him happy enough to give me a few days off.

"Spectacular! That'll give you a win at this race no doubt. Oh, that reminds me! We have to study the other runners!"

He proceeded to give me all kinds of information on the other top fifteen runners who would be at this race. For every runner, he gave me all sorts of information, from fastest time to their preferred shoe brand. Apparently certain brands produce faster runners. I had no idea how any of this information benefited me. All I could do was run to the best of my abilities and I would be fine. There was no strategizing about other runners in track, at least to me anyway.

As soon as I started walking to my last class, the thought of Summer intruded my brain again. I knew I had to be impervious to this kind of stuff, but thinking of her brought me comfort. Still, it had been nice to have a break from my thoughts while I talked to Coach Brothers, even if it was at the cost of boredom from that pointless meeting.

I just wish I had enjoyed the break while it lasted.

I kept checking Summer's Instagram to see if she removed the pictures of her and Davy or the part in her bio that read DT with a heart next to it, but every time I checked the page, it was still there. I even kept an eye out for the two of them in the hallways after school. I really didn't want to see Davy again, but it would definitely be worth it if I saw him being ratted out by Summer for acting the way he did earlier.

But then, I actually did see Davy. He was driving home in his brand spanking new, jet black Jeep that he had made sure everyone on social media knew about. Unfortunately, his shotgun rider was Summer, who for the first time in my life, I did not want to see--at least not with him. I saw the car coming my way as I walked home, so I put my hood over my head and kept it down to avoid him stopping and making fun of me again. When they pulled up to a stop sign ahead of me, I looked up. Summer was laughing and acting as if Davy were an angel and hadn't done anything to me. Before their car went out of my sight, I saw Davy look over at Summer, smile, then kiss her hand.

Chapter 10

The next few weeks were an uneventful hell. Life was just generally bad. I had not had any other encounters with Summer, I only saw Shane once over Christmas break, and my dad was harder on me than ever after "graciously" giving me two days off from running. Just as my cut started to scab, my training was in full force again. I definitely felt out of shape during my first run since the accident, but running inside felt a lot better than running outside in the cold Michigan air. My dad was hesitant on buying me a gym membership, but when he heard that Coach Brothers recommended I run inside, he gave me a hundred dollars and sent me off.

Every day of Christmas break I was expected to go train at the city's local gym, even on Christmas and New Year's, but especially on New Year's. The mark of January 1, 2018, meant that my race was only four days away. My dad was pushing me even harder than usual, coming to the gym to time my runs and yell, "One more eight hundred!"

I'll have to admit, I was in the best shape of my life, but Christmas break was meant for an actual "break," not relentless running around an indoor track. When I finally got my run time down, I thought it was the perfect opportunity to persuade my dad not to come along to Ann Arbor. He was practically jumping in his shoes when the stopwatch read "1:59:04." Coach Brothers informed my father that the fastest time out of all my opponents was seven seconds longer than what I had just ran.

"Hey, so you aren't coming to Ann Arbor, right?" I said, taking off my shoes.

"Heck yeah, why wouldn't I?" he responded with his proud voice.

"Well, I just thought you wouldn't want to go back after, well you know..." I tried to sound as nice as possible.

"I think I can do it," he scoffed. "I'm a big boy."

"Okay," I accepted defeat. If I pushed it any further he would just get angry.

Like I mentioned earlier, Shane and I only hung out once the entire break, which was weird because we usually chilled 24/7 during school breaks. But this time, whenever I asked him to do something, he always claimed that he was busy and would never say what he was doing.

Even though I knew what Shane was really doing, I tried ignoring how much it hurt. I wanted to confront him, but I was either too busy running or too exhausted to argue. The one night we did hang out wasn't very entertaining because he was so occupied with Camilla and Davy.

Shane had gotten Madden '18 for Christmas and we were playing against each other, but every two minutes or so, he would pause the game to check his text messages from Camilla. After I finally beat him, 42-7, he put in Call Of Duty and searched a party from our school. When he saw Davy's gamertag, he joined right away.

"Sorry bro, but I gotta wreck this idiot real quick," he pleaded with me as I expressed my unapproval.

The countdown on the screen hit zero and then I saw a dozen soldiers running around a map shooting at each other.

"These are all people from our school?" I asked, accepting the rejection of Shane's attention.

"Yeah, man," he took a sip of a Pepsi as he gunned someone down.

"Who was that?" I asked.

"Quentin, haha," he said in the most robotic voice.

"Isn't he..."

"Wait! There he is!" Shane shushed me and pointed toward an Arab militia soldier with the gamertag DAVYTHEGOAT.

Shane's character ran up behind Davy's soldier and stabbed him right in the back, causing blood to splurt everywhere and a "+100" to appear on Shane's screen. He turned his mic on and yelled, "HAHA! SUCK IT, DAVY."

A few suspenseful seconds later, we heard Davy say, "Who let this kid in?"

Shane smiled as he ran in pursuit of Davy again. When he finally found him, Davy was ready and blew him into pieces with one shot.

The rest of the game was a back-and-forth battle between the two. When Davy got the last kill on Shane to give his team the win, he yelled, "The game first, Camilla next?"

Was Davy single? Under the Bro Code he had just disrespected Shane greatly, but all I could wonder was if that meant he and Summer had broken up. I opened my phone and went to Summer's profile. The same content uglified her page.

Meanwhile, Davy and Shane were arguing once again on Xbox Live, but someone finally kicked Shane out and he said, "That reminds me, I told Camilla I would take her to play laser tag tonight. Do you need a ride home?"

I hadn't talked to him since, and I didn't plan on it until after my race. I needed a break from him and I hoped he would realize how much HE misses me.

Sadly, Shane didn't text me at all over the next four days, but he made sure to post a picture a day with Camilla on Instagram. She wasn't bad looking at all, and was probably learning more English by the day, but I couldn't convince myself to like her. How could I? She had replaced

me.

Part Two - The Race

Chapter 11

The young man continued to type away on his computer as the sky outside gradually became lighter and the airport grew more and more busy. He paused his writing and looked at his computer's clock. He saw that Flight 305 was scheduled to leave in about an hour. To be sure, he took his headphones out and listened for the monotone updates constantly being replayed around the building. Listening intensely to tune out the noise of a screaming baby and a woman arguing with someone on the phone, he was able to hear a robotic-like voice announcing plane departure times.

"Los Angeles, California. Flight 279. Fifteen minutes to departure."

"Phoenix Arizona. Flight 284. Twenty minutes to departure."

"Kansas City, Missouri. Flight 293. Thirty minutes to departure."

"Atlanta, Georgia. Flight 299. Fifty-one minutes to departure."

Nope, nope, nope, nope, the man thought in his head, annoyed.

"Raleigh, North Carolina. Flight 305. Fifty-nine minutes to departure."

The man nodded his head in confirmation, plugged his headphones back in his ears, and started typing once again.

January 5 was supposed to be my first day back to school after a very long and boring Christmas break. Instead, I would spend my day in Ann Arbor with hundreds of other runners. I wondered if any others were in the same boat as me. Surely, there had to be at least one or two, right?

The only time my father ever came in my room was when he had to wake me up for early track races. I'm pretty sure I could have hidden drugs or alcohol and he would have never found anything. It was so rare that when he did come into my room he almost looked out of place, like a criminal in a little girl's princess-themed room. The feeling must have been mutual because all he would do was walk in, turn on my light, and walk back out.

After hiding underneath my blanket from the searing light, I slowly eased my eyes out from under the covers to adjust them to the sudden change. When I finally got my eyes to completely focus, I looked over and read the time on my alarm clock: 3:28 a.m.

I thought waking up at 5 a.m. was bad enough, but 3:30 a.m.?

I rolled over and helplessly sprawled out across my bed. For some reason, maybe because of how early it was, I couldn't stop thinking about my mom.

What would life be like if she was still here?

Would I still run track?

Would I LIKE running track?

I found it very unsettling to miss someone who I had never spoken to. It was the same way I felt about Summer. I liked to think that my mom would have given me advice about Summer. She could have told me how to make a move, or tell me the right things to say. You know, tell me what girls want guys to do. Heck, maybe my dad would still be a good person and he could have helped me himself.

"URIAH?" my dad yelled from downstairs, breaking my train of thought.

"Coming!" I yelled back, annoyed. He definitely did not need to get me up at 3:30 when we didn't even have to leave until four. I could get ready in ten minutes.

I decided to try and get some more sleep in the car and I brought a pillow along. I sat in the passenger seat, laid my pillow behind my head on the seat, and closed my eyes. When my dad got in the car, I heard the ignition start and felt the car shift into drive. The town was so still that the only movement was light snow falling from the sky. When I opened my eyes to re-adjust my pillow, I could see nothing but our car's headlights on the road. There were no other vehicles on the road, no businesses open yet, and no house lights on. We didn't meet another vehicle until we merged onto the freeway and saw a couple of semi-trucks.

After a few failed attempts at falling asleep, I fought to overcome the exhaustion and headache from waking up so early. It was one of those days where nervousness overruled tiredness. In just three and a half hours I could possibly be getting ready for a race; it all depended on what pool I was in. There were eight groups of 800-meter runners and when I got to the track I would find out where I was placed. Pool A raced first right at 8 a.m., and Pool H raced at 12:30 p.m. I had learned this from the ginormous stack of papers that Coach Brothers had given me about the race.

With every waning minute the sun penetrated into the eastern part of the sky. Correspondingly, more and more morning commuters began to swarm the roads. Before I knew it, it was 6 a.m. About two hours down, only one more to go. Meanwhile, all this time, neither my dad or I spoke. The only sound in our car was a classic rock station that was turned down low enough to where you could barely hear it.

When the clock read half past six, I silently groaned at the fact that I ordinarily would just be getting up around this time. You know, like a normal person. I leaned my head against my pillow and thoughts of every possible situation that could happen at the track race invaded my mind and took over. I pictured myself barely winning and my dad and coach being slightly disappointed, but still happy. I imagined winning by a landslide and being able to stop somewhere on the way home. And while I tried to ignore this last thought, I also envisioned myself having an off day and losing to some scrub. I would, honestly, be terrified to ride the entire way back home with my dad. He would be so mad that he might possibly make me ride home with Coach Brothers, and I think I would rather do that. That's saying something.

All of these thoughts spiraled around my head until I dozed off into a light sleep. After what seemed like forever, yet such a short time, I woke up to my dad operating the car around a buzzing city, filled with college students, hospitals, campus buildings, and athletic stadiums.

We were here. I was in Ann Arbor.

Chapter 12

As our car maneuvered its way around the streets of Ann Arbor, I could almost see the internal war raging inside my father's head. I knew he was excited for my race, but being here was a painful reminder of the disappointment he had experienced in this very city so many years ago.

After dozens of turns, left and right, along with many stoplights, we rolled into the parking lot of a large, dome building with a giant, yellow "M" on its side. It was five minutes until seven, and the parking lot was flooded with runners who were walking to the sign-in area, some who stared at us in hopes of intimidating me, and others who were cool and minded their own business.

As soon as our car engine shut off, my dad was practically out of the car. He closed his door and pulled his pants up in a really cocky way, knowing I was the best runner there and wanting to make sure everyone else knew it too. He strolled arrogantly along my side to the sign-in line, ignoring all the stares and whispers. I was used to people whispering about me because no one really liked racing against me, but I have to think some of them were talking about my face too. I really had done some damage in that icy fall. It was really weird; everyone knew me here, but no one back in my own town knew who I was.

Just as I began feeling really uncomfortable from all the staring, I heard someone yelling my name. At first I didn't realize they were talking to me, but then I turned and saw one of my buddies from Indiana, Jeffrey, jogging my way. He was a friend who I had met through track and only ever saw at races.

"Hey! What's going on, my man?" Jeffrey gave me a handshake. He was really energetic for it to be so early in the morning.

I looked up at Jeffrey, who was a few inches taller than me, and smiled, "Hey, how's it going? I didn't know you would be here!"

"Yeah, man! Ouch!" he looked closer at the scar on my face.

I ended up telling him the whole story and when I was finished, my dad asked, "What are you running today?"

Jeffrey's brown eyes bounced back and forth between my dad, who was smiling from ear to ear, and me. My father loved Jeffrey, which I found really odd. I never could pinpoint why he was so enthralled with him.

"Yeah," Jeffrey smiled. "Gonna try the 800 today."

"Really?" my dad and I said simultaneously.

I began speaking again, but my dad cut me off.

"That's what Uriah is running!"

"No kidding?" Jeffrey sunk his shoulders and laughed. "I wanted to win today!"

"Hey, you're a beast, man. You'll do great!" I pushed his shoulder jokingly.

"Yeah, and anyway he needs a challenge!" my dad said, pointing to me. I turned and gave Jeffrey an apologetic look.

Jeffrey's dad called for him from another line and exchanged a wave with my dad.

"Well, gotta go! See you on the track!" Jeffrey waved and ran back to his line.

"Nice kid," my dad's voice trailed off as we finally reached the sign-in table.

An African-American woman with curly black hair greeted us as we walked up.

"Hi! Welcome to the 16th annual Ann Arbor Track Invitational! If you could, fill out your name, school, grade, and event then we'll give you your information and you'll be on your way."

My dad immediately took the paper and filled it out quickly in his surprisingly neat handwriting. The lady took the paper, looked up and down a list of runners, and then peeled off our nametags and gave us the information regarding my race. We both reached for the papers, but my dad snagged them and started walking inside. I wanted to tell him to give me MY papers, but he was in his glory and I couldn't kill the only true happiness he had in a very long time.

I stared at him and then the paper, trying to figure out when I would be racing. Finally, after a brief examination of all the printed words, he blurted out, "Class B. You'll be racing at about nine."

"Cool," I relaxed. It wasn't an ideal time, but at least it wouldn't be in less than an hour.

"Spatkin (Jeffrey), McDaniels, Schut, Kent, Cambridge, Gaudy, Samuels, Hoebbel," he read out the last names of the other runners in my pool, all who I barely recognized. The only face I could put with those names was Alex Gaudy, someone I had raced against a few times. Besides that, all I knew about these names were if they were good at running or not. I surmised that my only competition in Pool B was Scott Hoebbel, who I would probably still beat by a landslide.

After pushing our way through the facility's crowded hallways, we finally reached the track. It smelled of a fresh spring day, even though we were in the middle of a very cold winter. All across the track oval and the surrounding artificial grass were runners doing stretches, running small sprints, or fueling up for the day. We located the tent labeled "800 Meter Pool B" pretty close to where we entered the dome.

Underneath, I immediately saw Coach Brothers stuffing his face with a donut and flagging us down. My dad pointed and smiled as we made our way over to the tent. Coach Brothers rubbed his hands to free them of the white powder from his not-so-healthy breakfast, then shook my dad's hand.

"Rich! Long time no see!" he said with a powdered sugar smile. He was in his glory all right, a track race AND donuts. Ironically, no one on our team had ever seen Coach Brothers run.

"Hey there, coach! Way too long…" my dad agreed. He only acted like a normal father at track races. Why couldn't he be like that at home?

While the two talked about track in so much depth that they could have written an encyclopedia, I observed all of the other runners. Normally I would be intimidated by this many people who did the same thing as me, but I knew I was better than all of them. I know that sounds cocky, but it is the truth. You don't get intimidated when you are the one feared on the track.

I looked at all the other tents labeled with different events and pools until I found 800 Meter Pool A. I squinted my eyes to try and make out who was under the tent. I only spotted a few students; the rest must have been stretching for their race. But, one of the kids under the tent was exactly who I was looking for.

Nolan Hightower.

Nolan is the biggest jerk I've ever competed against. Once in Indianapolis during a race, he cleated my calf from the back when he, as he said, "took a longer stride." Luckily, it was in the very beginning of the race so I was able to catch up and beat him, barely, but after I slowed down, I dropped to the ground for an athletic trainer to attend to my bloody leg. I had to be taken to an emergency room and needed six stitches as a result of his unethical move. I traced my fingers along the scar he had inflicted on my right calf as I watched his every move. I hoped he would advance just so I could beat him again.

When I turned back to my dad and coach, their attention had turned to the man with a microphone in the center of the track. Apparently it was time to go over all the rules, procedures, and events. The man was on a stand, attracting runners, players, and coaches like moths to a bright light.

I walked with my father and coach toward the man as he continued talking about the bathroom locations. When we finally got as close as possible, the man started explaining the procedure for the events.

"We will have four different events today. The 200 meter, the 400 meter, the 800 meter, and the 1,600 meter races. Each event will have seven different pools, A through H, and the winner from every pool will automatically advance to finals to decide first place overall. Let me remind everyone to have good sportsmanship. Let's have a great day! Good luck!" the man proudly stated into his microphone.

Immediately after he stopped talking, everyone retreated back to their tents as a woman's voice started calling out the first race, "First up is 800 meters, Pool A. On deck: 400 meters, Pool A."

"Here, come on, let's get some good seats!" my dad said as he raced off toward our tent. He was like a little kid on Christmas day.

When we got back to the tent, my dad grabbed three white, plastic chairs and we set them up as closely to the track as possible. By the time we were settled into our spots, the runners were getting positioned at the start line. I looked at my phone. 8:01 a.m. I then looked over at my dad, who was resting his head on his intertwined hands. He whispered over to Coach Brothers, who nodded and pointed to the start line. The race had started.

Nolan had gotten off to a slow start and was in the middle of the pack. One kid that I didn't recognize had a couple steps of a lead over all the other runners, who were all clustered together, with one straggler behind them.

My dad turned to me and asked, "You want Nolan to win this?"

"Definitely," I said right away, watching the race very intensely.

As the runners got farther away from me, it became hard to tell who was who. When they finally came around their first lap, Nolan had pulled ahead of everyone and the kid who had taken the early lead was now almost in last place. He must have started out running way too hard and tired himself out. Rookie mistake.

When the runners passed us, it was pretty clear that Nolan was going to win. I looked up at the clock and the time was at about about a minute and forty-five seconds. I found this comforting because it meant that even Nolan wouldn't end up with a good score. When everyone had finally crossed the finish line, I saw Nolan's name at the top with a time of 2:14:59. Nolan raised his arms in the air in victory as he slowed down and stopped.

My dad looked over at me and nodded. I smiled back at him. We went back to our tent to relax for half an hour before my pool would be called on deck. I ate a banana and kept taking slow sips of water. I felt a little bit nervous, but I had done this race so many times before that I also felt very confident.

Finally, after distractedly watching a couple other races, the lady's voice sounded through a microphone, "Next on deck: 800 meter, Pool B." I checked the time on my phone before I threw it in my bag and headed to the on-deck area. The time read 8:56 a.m. When Jeffrey, the other runners, and I all entered the on-deck area, the lady did a roll call like a substitute teacher would do at school. When she finally read my name, I raised my hand and said, "here." Everyone turned to look at me with anxious looks on their faces, all except Jeffrey, who was smiling.

After the race ahead of us ended, we were quickly escorted to the starting line. I was in the second lane from the very inside, which meant I was behind almost everybody. Jeffrey positioned himself on the very most outward lane and I gave my legs a quick last-minute shake. The woman's voice then came over the microphone, "Runners, please take your mark." I put my leg on the starting block, as did everybody else, and waited.

My eyes were closed with my head facing straight down at the ground as I listened for the fake gun to sound.

Everything in the whole building seemed to go silent. My body was completely still, ready to leap into action. Just as I opened my eyes… "Bang!"

We were off.

Chapter 13

The first sound I heard after the initial gunshot was the lady's voice calling a 400-meter race to the deck. All at once, everything had gone silent, then suddenly erupted. Cheers from coaches, parents, and teammates roared throughout the entire building as we all took off. It didn't take me long to catch the two kids nearest to my lane and they soon fell off my radar. I only looked at who was ahead of me, and I knew that in no time I should catch up.

Just about 200 meters in, I was already creeping up on Alex Gaudy, who had taken the early lead. Everyone else, including Jeffrey, was behind me, therefore I had no interest in them. My main goal was to steadily gain on Alex and then really take off for the big lead.

With every waning step I could feel and see myself gaining distance. Instead of looking at the spectators, clock, or other runners behind me, I focused on Alex's shoes--blue Adidas that seemed to be color coordinated with the rest of his outfit. I looked at his shoes because looking at something else might distract me; Coach Brothers had taught me that.

But as we turned the last corner before reaching the starting point again, I couldn't look at his shoes anymore. If I did, my head would have needed to be turned a whole 180 degrees. I was now ahead of him, taking long and powerful strides with every single step. My heartbeat was pounding in my ears with my steady breaths.

When I first passed him, Alex was visible through my peripheral vision but soon after, he was no longer near me. The only footsteps I could hear were my own as I hit the halfway mark. I rounded the corner, where my dad and coach were watching from, and I was pretty sure I heard my dad screaming, "LET'S GO!"

Normally at this point in the race I felt at least a bit of fatigue, but none was present this time. My breathing methods were spot on and I showed no sign of slowing down. Perhaps every pain, struggle, and stress in the past month was just unleashing itself as I ran like never before. The empty track ahead of me seemed to be getting smaller and smaller at a very quick pace. Before I knew it, the finish line was only about 50 meters away and I pushed every last bit I had in me as I strived one last time to cross the finish line.

First place.

It took some time to slow down my acceleration, but when I finally came to a stop I looked back and saw the other runners all bunched together like a dozen flowers crossing the finish line. In awe, I turned and looked at the clock. Next to the white "1" was my name with the time of 1:54:98. My dad and Coach Brothers were going to be ecstatic. Even I'll admit that I was pretty pumped at that good of a time. It was pretty close to the world record holder's time.

"And the winner of the 800 meter, Pool B class, by a landslide, Uriah Peterson!" the woman announced with emotion for the first time all day.

I walked over and slapped Jeffrey's hand, and he bent over and acted like I was a god he worshipped. I modestly thanked him and gave him a last handshake before he went back to his coach.

When I got to the tent, my dad and coach, undoubtedly, were standing with the proudest looks on their faces. I was used to winning, but for some reason this one felt extra special. I needed this race at this point in my life; nothing else brought me happiness. And this was only the first race. The championship run would feel even better.

"Absolute monster race, Uriah," my dad was almost giggling in excitement. "I just hope you saved some energy for the next race."

"Yeah, heck of a race, kid!" Coach Brothers patted me on the back.

"Thanks," I said, still somewhat out of breath. "I should be good to go. I feel amazing."

"I love to hear that!" my dad exclaimed as he walked with a winning swagger.

We sat back in our chairs at the tent and almost every kid in my pool came and shook my hand before they left. Their day was over.

Some of these poor kids drove hours just to lose to me, I thought with a silent laugh.

When I realized I sounded just like my dad, guilt flooded my conscious for thinking such a cocky thing and I was glad I didn't actually say it out loud to anyone. My dad restocked my body's needs by giving me water to drink and energy-producing foods while we watched the next races. We only spectated the other, unimportant-to-me races, and then carefully studied any 800-meter races. By 11 a.m., four of the seven championship race spots for the 800 had been claimed, and no one had even come close to my time.

A boiling sensation of excitement bubbled in my stomach. I couldn't wait to have my dad act pleasant toward me again for a few days. And, hopefully I would receive at least a little bit of recognition from someone at school and, if not, Shane would always be there to congratulate me. That reminded me, I had to text him.

Me: I just got done with my first race. Personal record of 1:54:98, beat everyone by a landslide. I will race against that kid who spiked my calf a while back.

A few minutes later, I felt the buzz of my phone and immediately checked the notification.

Shane: Freaking dope, dude. Good luck in the 'ship!

Me: Thanks, man. I'll let you know.

I then started typing another text to tell him that my friend Jeffrey was here but the start of the 800 meter, Pool E, race distracted me.

By half past noon, the entire 800-meter championship race was set. The fastest time besides my own was the winner of Pool H, who ran an impressive 2:03:39. A small amount of worry slipped its way into my mind and I started overthinking everything that could go wrong. I could get super tired, or I could become super rusty and not run a good race. I could have set the bar too high and disappointed my dad. Worst of all, I could flat out lose to the kid I absolutely loathed. When the worries started compressing together in my mind to form anxiety, a simple reminder from my dad strangely calmed everything.

"Pool H winner will still be tired when you race again. Other than him, you have no one else to worry about," he ensured me with nervous excitement in his voice.

I nodded my head as I listened to the man who was now announcing the times of the championship races.

"At 1 p.m., finalists for the 200-meter event will race. At 1:15 p.m., finalists for the 800-meter event will race. At 1:30 p.m., finalists for the 400-meter event will race. And finally, at 2 p.m., finalists for the 1,600-meter event will finish out our day together. Again, good luck to all of our runners!"

So I would be racing at 1:15. I checked my phone and I saw that the race would begin in roughly thirty minutes. That wasn't enough time for the Pool H winner to physically and mentally recover to race that fast of a time again.

My dad seemed to be thinking the exact same thing because he turned to me and gently squeezed my shoulder, "This is easy money, Uriah."

As preparations for the first race began on the track, many event workers started tearing down the tents around the track. A lady in a maize shirt was yelling loudly for all finalists to meet in the grass area inside the middle of the track. We all followed orders and carried our belongings to the center area, where the fastest runners had to wait. Every other person was asked to go in the stands.

My dad was outraged with the idea of not being able to coach or motivate me before the run, but he decided not to make a scene in case it would jeopardize my chances. Once he reached the stands, he yelled, "Do what you always do! You got it, kid!"

I was all alone now, which wasn't foreign to me. I sat silently and observantly as I tried to study my opponents. Only getting more nervous from watching the other runners, I checked the time on my phone: **12:58.**

The 200-meter runners were now being called individually to the start line, with the entire crowd generically clapping for each runner to be polite.

After everyone was introduced and clapped for, the runners, as the saying goes, took their marks. A very long pause echoed throughout the silent building as the anticipation for the gunshot loomed. Finally after long suspension, the gunshot sounded and the runners took off. It was a very quick race compared to mine, and a short stubby kid named Stewart Malcolm took the win and celebrated atop

the podium. Everyone in the crowd clapped for Stewart, but a

genuine, loud cheer came from a group who must have been

his teammates, coaches, and family.

"Next race will be the 800 meter in five minutes!" the

lady's voice rang. The sound waves from her microphone

entered my stomach and hatched eggs of excitement that

spread throughout my whole body. Now was my chance, my

time.

The next time the lady spoke I knew the race was

about to start. She repeated the same procedure and

introduced everyone. I silently booed Nolan Hightower when

his name was called out. I was last, and maybe it was my

arrogance, but my cheers for me seemed to be more

genuine than anyone else's.

"Runners, will you please take your marks?" her voice

said smoothly.

We all took our spots and waited for the gunshot. The

time that passed until the gunshot seemed way too long, like

when the winner is revealed on a reality TV show. I tried

being patient with whoever decided to pull the trigger. I closed and opened my eyes about three different times before a loud noise erupted through the air and every single runner sprung from their block and took off.

Everything from that first jump soon became a giant blur. All I remember after the gunshot was one step, a snapping sound, and the tumbling of my body to the ground as I clenched my knee in pain.

Chapter 14

This was easily the most painful injury I had ever had, and believe me, I had encountered plenty by that time in my life. Like in the first grade when I fell off the monkey bars after trying to impress a cute girl and broke my arm in three places. A couple years later, I woke up in the middle of the night with sharp pains all throughout my sides and back and eventually passed a kidney stone. And, of course, just a few weeks ago was the big slip-and-fall on the ice incident with my face. While all three of these injuries produced immense discomfort, not one of them compared to the pain I was feeling now in my left knee. The burning sensation was unbearable, like my knee had snapped and was hanging loose from my femur. Through teary vision, I looked down at my leg to see if the pain matched reality.

To my surprise, my knee looked perfectly normal. There were no signs that correlated with the pain I was feeling in at that moment. I was trying to test the movement of my knee when two sets of hands were suddenly at my side, rushing frantically to get me off the track. I could see from my peripheral vision that the other runners were making their way around to the starting point again.

"Okay," a voice said calmly but quickly. "I need you to take the upper part of his body and on three we will move him to the grass."

One set of hands cradled my body from hip down and the other lifted my upper half and they carried me off to safety, while I still clenched my knee in howling pain. As soon as they laid me down, my vision became clearer and I could see two athletic trainers, a man and a women, at my side doing everything they could do to help.

"Where does it hurt the most?" the girl asked.

What a dumb question. I think anyone could have figured it out just by taking a quick glance.

I pointed to my left knee and they both turned their attention to my left side.

"Can you explain the pain?" she asked.

"It feels like my knee completely twisted and broke off," I whimpered.

They exchanged a worried glance and I knew that couldn't mean anything good. I turned my head away from the trainers to see my dad and Coach Brother's running across the track to the grass where I was being attended to.

"What happened?" Coach Brothers asked frantically.

"What went wrong?" my dad asked the male trainer. Of course he would try to blame this all on me. He wasn't even concerned about the amount of pain I was feeling.

The trainer shook his head in obvious frustration toward my dad and said, "Nothing. Just happens sometimes."

"Can you move it at all?" the girl asked. I tried bending my knee, but the pain was too much to bear.

Both of the trainers were now feeling around my knee. With every touch, rub and press, my leg seared with pain, causing me to wince. The female trainer clicked a button on her radio and spoke to someone on the other line, "Hey, I'm going to need you to call an ambulance, but in the meantime, I need some ice over here as soon as possible."

My heart started pounding with the same intensity that I felt in my knee.

Ambulance? I thought. *Is it really that bad?*

"Okay, Uriah," she looked me in the face. "We are going to take you to the hospital but while we wait for the ambulance, we're going to try and make you as comfortable as possible."

I let out a large, painful sigh. I knew I should have been more appreciative of the help they were giving me, but I was in too much pain and the race I had planned on winning just finished. It should have been me holding up the trophy in celebration, not Nolan Hightower.

"Sir, we are going to need you to give us your attention," the guy said after he noticed me fixated on Nolan.

I turned my head and somehow a bolt of pain erupted throughout my entire leg.

"What grade are you in?" the female trainer asked.

"Tenth," I answered shortly. I turned and looked at my dad, who was showing no emotion, just a lot of disappointment. If I wasn't in so much pain, I would have been furious with him. My leg felt like it had been shredded and all he cared about was that I didn't win the race. I'll admit, knowing Nolan won instead of me sucked, but my father didn't even show the tiniest bit of sympathy toward me.

"Wow, and I hear you're such a good runner!" she said, pretending like she was interested. I knew she couldn't care less; it was just one of those doctor communication methods.

"Ah, here," she said once one of her coworkers arrived with ice.

I didn't bother watching as she applied the ice, but I didn't have to. The sensation I felt was a mix of relieve from the coldness, yet pain from the pressure of the ice on my knee.

"How does that feel?" she asked.

"Okay," I was drowned out by the sounds of the 1600-meter race starting.

"Alright, hang in there, Uriah. The ambulance will be here any minute."

She got up and started asking my dad and coach questions. I tried eavesdropping, but the only thing I was able to hear was, "Has he had any history with…"

The male trainer was still crouching by my side. He seemed to be the lady's assistant or intern or something, but it really hadn't concerned me at the time. Just as the silence between us got very awkward, the lady returned with two paramedics and a stretcher. They didn't seem to be in a hurry, which made me feel slightly better. Instead, they were asking her as many questions as imaginable. After the lengthy conversation, one of the paramedics finally spoke to me.

"Okay, sir, we are going to place you on this stretcher and take you to the hospital. This may be painful but it will be short."

Slowly, the two EMTs picked me up and placed me on an oddly comfortable stretcher, like the ones you see on television.

As soon as I was securely in place on the stretcher, they began pushing me off the track. My dad and coach had been sent off to get my belongings and were told to meet us at Ann Arbor Children's Hospital. As I sat upright, I observed hundreds of eyes watching me be rolled off of the track, and then everyone in the building stood up and started clapping for me. I could feel my face becoming warm as I put my hand up to acknowledge all the people who were kind enough to show me that much support.

When we entered the hallway, the loud sound of cheers coming from the track were muffled, soothing my ringing ears. The paramedics seemed like they knew this place inside and out as they made it to the parking lot in an incredibly short amount of time. An ambulance was waiting for us not too far from where my father had parked earlier that morning. The doors opened revealing another paramedic, who was preparing the inside for my arrival. After I got situated in the back of the vehicle, I heard the engine turnover and start to hum.

"How is the pain?" one of the paramedics asked as the ambulance started driving away.

"It's still pretty bad," I said with my eyes closed.

I had never been in an ambulance before, but I always imagined it differently. It seemed to drive just like a normal vehicle would, maintaining the speed limit, and periodically stopping. I had imagined it would be very chaotic with a siren going off, but none of that was happening. The two paramedics sat by my side, calmly checking basic health measurements, like my temperature, blood pressure, and heart rate.

The pain was so overpowering that I tried comforting myself by asking, "So, my injury isn't too serious, right? I mean otherwise the siren would be going off, right?"

"Not necessarily," a man with wide, hazel eyes shook his head.

When I gave him a worried look he continued, "What I mean is, your life isn't in danger, but your leg seems to be in very poor shape."

"What is it?" I curiously asked.

"That's not for us to speculate. I'm pretty sure you will have a MRI tonight."

"Okay," I responded, offended. Everyone in the healthcare field, while being super knowledgeable and amazing at what they do, was sometimes very annoying.

"Do you play any other sports?" he asked.

"No, just track," I replied, trying to take my mind off the pain again, but it was difficult when I was being asked about the very thing that caused my injury.

"Ah, I see. So you enjoy running, I presume? I'm not much of a runner myself."

"I like to run, but not when I'm forced."

"Forced?"

"My dad was a track runner in high school and college, so I've basically been made to run my entire life and it really, really sucks."

"Oh, I see. If it helps at all, I can almost guarantee you won't be running for a long, long time," he half smiled. "Alright, we must be here!"

The vehicle came to a stop and soon after, the doors opened. I lifted my head and saw red letters above the entrance that read **Emergency Room** with a nurse in all blue standing below holding a clipboard.

The medics all worked together to get my stretcher on the ground as gently as possible. As soon as a couple other nurses came outside to bring me in, the paramedics had already taken off. I didn't even get a chance to say thank you.

"Hi!" a young nurse with a big smile shook my hand. "I am so sorry to hear about your leg, but we are going to be doing the best we can to take care of you. My name is Stacy and we are going to check you into a room. If you have any questions feel free to ask."

Chapter 15

I had no idea what time it was, only that my leg hurt badly and my dad was taking forever to arrive. A nurse stopped in occasionally to check up on me and have me rate my pain on a scale of one to ten. I told her eight every single time. With some help from the nurses, I changed into my hospital gown and socks, which were actually super comfortable. The only thing I could do now was wait. A nurse came in to tell me I had a MRI scheduled for 6 p.m., but I had no idea how long away that was from now.

I wanted to text Shane and tell him everything, but my phone was in my bag with my dad, who still hadn't arrived at the hospital. It wouldn't surprise me if he was sitting in the waiting room grieving the fact that I hadn't won, not that I was seriously injured.

It doesn't feel right to say that I didn't win, but it's not like I really lost. I didn't get more than two steps on the ground before I collapsed. To make matters worse, the winner for the day was my enemy, Nolan Hightower. I would have been fine if ANYONE but him had won. He just didn't deserve it, not the way he raced.

"Hi, Uriah!" Stacy walked in, smiling. "Still feeling like an eight?"

"Yes, still feeling like an eight," I repeated for what seemed like the millionth time.

"Okay, well in about a hour we are going to be moving you to the first floor for your MRI," Stacy announced.

"Great, thank you," I said as she started to leave the room. "Wait!"

She peeked her head around the corner and asked, "Yes?"

"Is my dad here?" I questioned.

She checked over her clipboard and then replied, "Yes! He's in the waiting room. Want me to go fetch him?"

So, he was doing the exact thing I had suspected. Figures.

"No," I whispered, shaking my head. "It's fine."

She nodded her head and took off.

The hour until my MRI was one of the most boring of my entire life. My only entertainment was occasional throbs of pain in my leg, resulting in me asking for more medication. Finally, after sixty long minutes, Stacy and a male nurse walked in, flipped up the sides on my bed, and started transporting me to the first floor.

Oddly enough, I loved the hospital. Something about it made me feel so safe and clean, even though I knew hospitals were, in fact, one of the dirtiest places.

In transport though, I realized how awful this place really is. I rolled by countless rooms with patients who looked so miserable it even made me depressed. I thought I had it bad, but after seeing all these hopeless eyes staring right back at me, I was thankful that my leg injury wasn't life threatening.

As we rolled into the Radiology Department, Stacy asked me, "Have you ever had a MRI?"

"No, but I've heard it's really claustrophobic. Is that true?"

"Yes, for some," Stacy told me. "You just have to lay still while this big machine takes a bunch of detailed pictures of your body. MRI stands for Magnetic Resonance Imaging."

"Well, that's soothing," I said sarcastically and she laughed.

I hadn't really been able to determine whether or not I liked her, but when she laughed at my joke I decided she was pretty cool. That's not even to mention the fact that she was a babe. She looked to be in her mid-twenties and had long black hair, green eyes, and perfect teeth. Because of how attractive she was, it had embarrassed me earlier when she had seen my salmon-colored underwear while I was changing into my hospital gown.

We finally reached the MRI room and Stacy knocked on the door. A few seconds later, an older man with white hair and a beard opened the door. He looked like a typical doctor, suited up in scrubs with a stethoscope hanging around his neck.

"Is this Uriah?" he asked in an unusually high voice.

"It is!" Stacy responded. "Uriah, this is James. He will be running your MRI today."

I nodded and shook James' hand.

"Alright, Stacy, thank you. I can take it from here," James said politely and Stacey left the room.

After asking to make sure I had nothing magnetic on or inside me, James moved me to the MRI machine and stuck headphones over my ears. He asked me what my favorite genre of music was and I quickly said rap.

I heard a door shut behind me and the MRI machine began to run soon after, just as a song came on through my headphones. I had started mouthing the words to the beginning of the song when the music stopped and I heard James' voice through the headphones.

"Alright, Uriah, make sure you lie completely still throughout the entire scan. It will be about 40 minutes." Then, the song came back on.

Turns out that it is a lot harder to stay completely still than you'd think. A few songs into the scan I had already started feeling jittery, like energy was slowly building up inside of me and I needed to burst. The machine was making loud noises as it spun around and around my leg. I'm not claustrophobic, but I was ready for this to be over. I had the type of nervous system where my body had to always be moving in one way or another.

I had no way to keep track of time except through the music I was listening to. I counted five songs that were probably about three or four minutes long. That meant I still had a while to go. Eventually the music calmed my jitters and I became somewhat comfortable, but then the music turned off and the machine began slowing down.

"Great job, Uriah. I'll be there in a second to get you out of there," James spoke to me through the headphones, promising to switch me from the MRI machine back to my hospital bed.

"Alright, I am going to process these for you as quickly as I can and you should have your results in the morning."

"Sounds good. Thank you," I waved as Stacy knocked on the door to wheel me back to my room for the night.

Of course, I didn't sleep very well. I was awakened by nurses entering my room every couple hours, and the sharp pains running through my leg didn't help my restlessness.

My father had decided to drive back home and get his work laptop while the doctors analyzed my MRI and decided what to do next. I was angry for two reasons. The biggest being that he wasn't sticking to his son's side during a tough time, but also because he hadn't thought to bring me my phone. I had no idea what the time was. I asked one of the night shift nurses if she could bring in a clock for me and she pointed out that there was a clock right behind my bed.

"Oh, sorry," I blushed, covered by the darkness in the room.

"You're fine!" she laughed.

I woke up for good around 7 a.m. the next morning. Exactly one day ago I was just arriving at the track, talking to Jeffrey. If only I had known that twenty-four hours later I wouldn't be getting ready for school, but would be in a hospital bed in Ann Arbor.

Wait, my heart skipped a beat. *If that was one day ago, I've probably lost all my Snapchat streaks.*

I knew that should have been the least of my worries, but I was approaching the glorious one-year streak with Shane...

At around 7:30, Stacy walked into my room.

"Oh, good, you're up!" she said really peppy for it being this early in the morning.

"Yeah," I tried fixing my hair, embarrassed at how I probably looked. "So did you get my results back?"

"Yes," she spoke in a bad-news-bearing tone. "Dr. Steinberg will be in here any minute to speak with you."

"Okay, sounds good."

I was annoyed she couldn't just come on out and tell me, but this was Stacy and I had grown to really like her.

A few minutes later, a tall man with glasses walked into the room.

"Uriah?" he asked.

"That's me," I sat up.

"Good to meet you! Now, let's talk about that knee."

"Finally," I was ready to find out at last. "Let's hear it."

"One of the ligaments in your knee has torn. Unfortunately, the ligament is your Anterior Cruciate Ligament, otherwise known as your ACL."

He didn't have to say anymore; I knew all about ACL tears. They were career ruiners for many athletes. Most professional athletes would miss a whole season after suffering an ACL tear. I just couldn't come to grips that actually I had torn mine. It didn't seem real.

"So, I'm assuming it will require surgery?" I asked Dr. Steinberg.

"Yes, you will need surgery. We have scheduled it for 10 a.m."

Chapter 16

My dad returned to the hospital just about an hour before my surgery. We spoke for the first time since my injury as a hospital crew prepared me for the procedure.

"How's it feeling?" he finally asked in an awkward tone, like parenting was a new concept to him. Then again, I wouldn't exactly call what he's done parenting; it was more of guardianship.

"Fine," I looked at the wall. I was still too angry to look him in the face.

"It's a shame," he stared at my leg marked for surgery. "Same type of thing happened to me, except I won't let this end your career."

"Yeah," I mumbled as I watched the anesthesiologist prep my arm for the sleep-inducing drugs.

"I mean, you are only a sophomore in high school, you still got plenty of--"

"Dad, can you not worry about running, for like two seconds? I'm about to have freaking surgery."

My dad appeared shocked that I had snapped at him. In embarrassment, he turned red and I recognized his facial expression as the one he usually made before he hit me. But, he was smart enough not to do or say anything with the anesthesiologist in the room, who I could tell felt very awkward..

"Well, good luck," he mumbled and walked out of the room.

My palms were sweaty and I felt as if the rest of my body was going to catch up with my ACL and explode. I didn't know if I could take two more years of this. But then again, if I didn't cooperate with his selfish ways my life would be miserable.

When Dr. Steinberg came in and told me the surgery was going to begin in fifteen minutes, I didn't have room for anger anymore. Nerves were taking over. I had never had a real surgery before. A year ago I had gotten my wisdom teeth out, but I didn't consider that real surgery. This time, I would be completely unconscious for a couple hours while they cut into my leg and reconstructed my knee. When I wake up, I would probably be in more pain than before, Dr. Steinberg explained to me. My palms were now sweaty, not from anger, but anxiety. My body began involuntarily shaking and I felt like I was going to throw up. The anesthesiologist noticed and calmed me by saying, "You should be feeling the anesthesia soon."

I nodded my head and closed my eyes. I hated this feeling, but surely it was normal, right? After a couple minutes, my body started feeling heavy and my surroundings became hard to focus in on. I couldn't see any details of anything, just mere blobs of the hospital room.

"I think it's working," I told the anesthesiologist.

"Well, that's good!" he smiled.

I thought anesthesia would make me forget about where or who I was, but it didn't. But I knew I must have been acting weird because they started treating me like a little kid.

Then, things went dark.

I was asleep, or was I? Can you still function while under anesthesia?

I opened my eyes, only to realize that I had just closed my eyes. I wasn't fully unconscious yet. I was able to adjust to my surroundings, where I found myself in a really creepy room that I had never seen before. It seemed really small in width but tall in height. I was lifted and placed on a cold, white surface. I looked around and hazily saw numerous doctors and all sorts of tools.

"Are you, you, you going to use that one me?" I could barely speak now.

"How're you feeling, Uriah?" Dr. Steinberg asked me.

"I feel... great! Just a little tired!" I couldn't keep my eyes open any longer.

"Well, that's normal. Now you just go to sleep and we are going to fix your leg!"

"MY LEG?" I screamed.

"Shhhh... yes, Uriah, yes!" he kept saying.

And then, just like that, I spiraled down and down into a pit of unconsciousness.

Chapter 17

I woke up in a completely different place than where I had passed out and I could feel myself crying even though I didn't feel any pain yet. I tried swallowing but it was almost impossible. I kept coming in and out of consciousness, every single time things becoming more clear to me.

The pain hit me all at once. My leg was throbbing like never before and the discomfort was almost unbearable. I felt the pain not only inside my knee, but along every bone, ligament, and muscle in my leg. Even my skin felt tight and achy.

At first, I had no idea where I was, as the room was completely unrecognizable. It was very dim so the light was easier for my eyes to adjust to and the space had a certain coziness that my previous room didn't have. As things became more and more clear, I realized I must be in the recovery room.

"How we doing?" Stacy walked in, frightening me at first.

"It hurts," I tried wiping the tears from my face so she wouldn't see.

"I know, unfortunately! We gave you some pain meds just before you woke up so it should be going away soon."

As she checked all my vital signs, the pain minimally subsided like she promised. When everything was clear, Stacy left without saying a word and came back with my dad a couple minutes later.

He looked me right in the face with a fake smile.

"How does it feel?" he asked.

"Not very good," I responded. My throat still found difficulty swallowing.

"Well, don't worry about anything but resting. We just gotta get you healed up for next season!"

Even though it wasn't exactly what he should have said, I could live with it. At least he tried to show that he cared about me, unlike the past twenty-four hours where he made everything all about him. My dad sat down next to me and pulled my phone out of his pocket. I grabbed for it right away and was surprised at how cold it was. I clicked the home button and it came to life, only a few percent lower than it had been yesterday. I was eager to see all of my notifications and especially messages from Shane that I could finally respond to. I saw that I had four unread messages.

Shane (4:52 p.m.): Hey, how'd it go?

Shane (6:22 p.m.): Hello?

Shane (8:59 p.m.): Alright....? Well, see you at school tomorrow.

Shane (8:01 a.m.): Seriously, bro, what's wrong? What did I do?

I couldn't type fast enough. I filled him in about the past twenty-four hours of my life, everything from the race, to the MRI, to the surgery. I even told him about the hot nurse, Stacy. He responded right away.

Shane: Wait, I've missed so much. You seriously tore your ACL, bro? And had surgery? That's freaking craaaaaazy.

We texted back and forth about the details of what happened until Stacy told me it was time for my father and I to meet with Dr. Steinberg, who would fill us in on the next steps. I quickly texted Shane.

Me: Hey, gotta go. Let you know when I get home.

Shane: Sounds good. I'll come over to visit ASAP.

It felt good to be close with Shane again. My surgery had made me lose track of time, which made it feel like our friendship was back to normal, texting each other back and forth telling stuff.

I set my phone on my lap while I was being transported to a regular room with my dad walking alongside. Dr. Steinberg was already waiting on us. He surveyed me as they wheeled me in.

"How's it feeling?" I was asked yet again.

"Better than before," my bed came to a stop. "Still hurts though."

"That's all we can ask for from here on out, improvement!" he smiled. "Now, dad, we have some information to relay."

My dad came out of a daze and nodded his head confusingly, like he had forgotten that he was still a father.

"We are going to wrap Uriah's leg very securely, first with leg wrap, then with a brace that will keep his leg in a straight position. When you leave in a few minutes, I expect him to be in the backseat of the car with his leg resting on the seat," he explained. My dad nodded, occasionally taking a glance at me.

"When you get home, no school for at least a week. After about seven days, see how you feel and then you can decide. Keep your leg brace on at all times, except when showering, which you cannot do for three days," Dr. Steinberg carefully explained. "We will send along a pair of crutches to help Uriah walk, but keep his mobility low for the next few weeks. We have called your pharmacy and have his meds all set up. For everything else, such as therapy and where to go next, your local doctor will be contacting you."

My dad and I both nodded even though Dr. Steinberg only seemed to be talking to him. We all shook hands, and then Stacy walked in and prepared me for my departure.

I was sad to leave Stacy, but happy to get out of the hospital. I never thought I would miss home this much. Stacy wheeled me out to the entrance, where my dad took control

of the wheelchair. He pushed me at a very fast pace, not

pausing to ask if the speed was okay.

It wasn't.

The sun was out and emitting warmth throughout the

winter air. It felt good to be outdoors again, like the air was a

refreshing cold drink on a warm summer day. It smelled like

spring and I wasn't sure if I had been inside too long, or if it

was actually just a really nice day.

"Where's your car?" I asked, looking for my dad's

vehicle.

"Should be over here," he said while fumbling for his

keys inside his coat pocket.

He clicked the unlock button and I searched for the

blinking lights. I scanned the whole parking lot, full of dozens

of cars, light poles, and numerous people, including two who

caught my eye. It was a man with a younger girl, who looked

oddly familiar. Still a little hazy from the anesthesia, I

searched every part of my brain to recall how I knew this girl,

then it hit me.

Oh crap.

She was the last person I wanted to see at this moment. I looked horrendous and felt terrible, but apparently God didn't care because walking in the parking lot alongside who I assumed was her father, wearing the black hat she always wore, was Summer Harris.

Part Three - The Romance

Chapter 18

The young man found himself running to catch his flight. He had gotten to the airport with plenty of time to spare, but writing had caused him to lose track of time. He wanted to make sure that he reached a certain point in his writing before he boarded the plane, and now he wasn't even sure that he would make it in time to board.

How could I be so stupid? he thought. *I'm finally doing this and now I'm going to screw it all up.*

He rounded a corner and ran toward the door under an electronic sign that read: **Flight 305: Raleigh, North Carolina.**

There was no one left waiting in line. He would be lucky if they hadn't already closed the door. As he ran with his laptop between his arms, he caught the lady who was starting to close the door.

"Please!" he struggled. "Please wait!"

Luckily, the lady heard him and gave him enough grace to stop the door.

When he finally got there, panting, the attendant looked very annoyed.

"You barely made it you know," she said, grouchily.

"I know, sorry, working on---" the young man responded.

"Name, please," she cut him off.

"Uriah. Uriah Peterson," he puffed.

"You got lucky. You can board."

She opened the door for him and he walked onto the plane, catching many dirty looks while he searched for his seat. When he finally found it near the back of the plane, he sat down, pulled out his laptop, and began writing again.

"Ladies and gentlemen, prepare for takeoff. Estimated flight time to Raleigh, North Carolina, three and a half hours."

With that, the airplane took off into the sky.

Chapter 19

The world's population is home to seven billion people and it literally could have been anyone walking in that Ann Arbor parking lot. It felt like fate was on my side for once. Out of all the odds, here was the love of my life, Summer Harris, walking toward me. I was hours away from my hometown, where I often had to put in a great deal of effort to even see her, and yet here she was, fifty feet away from me in that parking lot. This was finally my break, the crazy story I was convinced would never happen to me.

Yet, for very stupid reasons, I had no desire to talk to Summer. I had dreamed of an encounter with her, and even though it was basically waiting for me, I decided that this moment was not the right time. I was embarrassed at how I looked, and smelled, and the fact that my dad would be there made it a million times worse.

"Dad, go right," I said quietly, even though Summer was still a long distance away.

"Uh, why?" he asked suspiciously.

"Just, go right. I think I saw our car over that way," I pointed from my wheelchair.

"No, it's right over here. I just saw it," he pointed to our car, which Summer was walking by as we spoke. "You must still be high on those drugs."

The distance between Summer and us was getting rapidly smaller. Our encounter was inevitable. My stomach was viciously churning and I felt like I was about to hurl.

Not like this, not like this, not like this, I pleaded.

As our paths crossed, Summer quickly glanced at me and then looked away. At first I was relieved she hadn't noticed me, but when I realized she hadn't even recognized me, I was absolutely crushed.

But then, she did a double take.

"Hey!" she suddenly stopped and looked at me with a big smile on her face.

I could almost hear my heart pounding underneath my skin. *She said 'hey' to me!*
I was certain that I was nobody to her but the skinny sophomore who her boyfriend bullied.

"Hey, Summer!"

Worried thoughts flooded my brain. *Would she think I was creepy for knowing her name?*

"What are you doing? Oh my goodness, what happened to your leg?" she walked over and placed her hand on my brace, which sent a jolt of pain down my leg, but I really didn't care; this was Summer!

"I was competing in a track race yesterday and I tore my ACL," I said in a way that made me seem like a hero.

"Wow, I'm so sorry. That sucks!" she winced.

"School friend, Uriah?" my dad asked. I had completely forgot he was there.

"Yes!" Summer responded for me when I hesitated. "We usually just see each other in the halls, but we have a class together this semester. I was wondering why you weren't there yesterday."

We actually had a class together? Me and Summer Harris? And right now, she was talking to me as if we were really good friends, when in reality we had never spoken to each other.

"Really? What class?" I tried my best to keep my cool.

"Algebra 2," she responded.

She was much more beautiful up close. Her features were more distinct in close proximity. Her eyes, welcoming you in with every single blink. Her lips, a perfect shade of pink. Her luscious brown hair falling graciously over her shoulders. Her face, with no deformations or pimples, which was rare for a teenager.

"That's cool," I smiled. "It'll probably be a while until I'm back, though."

"Understandable," she nodded her head.

Gosh, she was so perfect, so nice... I had been right about her after all.

"Hey!" her dad yelled with excitement. I looked up at him, and like my own father, I had forgotten he was even there. Summer had the capability of driving everything else out of my mind when she was around.

What could have possibly made him blurt out like that? The answer to my question came after one quick look at the man. I recognized him immediately. He was the same guy who had been walking his dog and let me use his phone on the night I fell and injured my face. Crazy how things work sometimes.

"Aren't you..."

"The guy walking his dog a few weeks ago?" he smiled and nodded his head. "I wasn't sure if it was you at first but when I saw your scar, I knew it had to be you."

My dad and Summer shared the same confused look on their faces.

"Wait, dad," Summer looked back and forth between us. "It was Uriah that one night?"

Summer said my name like no one else did, majestically putting emphasis on the "UR."

"Small world, eh?" they simultaneously laughed in the same hereditary way.

"Well, we better be leaving! Got some healing to do," my dad was the buzzkill to the best encounter of my entire life.

"We do too," Summer smiled. "See you in school, Uriah. I hope you feel better!"

My dad rolled me away and I tried to cover the smile on my face, but I couldn't do it. I wanted to feel this way forever.

Stacy had told my dad the painkillers would probably knock me out on the car ride home and to make sure my leg stayed upright, but that wasn't a problem. I stayed awake the entire ride. I mean, how could I not? I had just officially talked to the girl I'd been dreaming about for weeks, and it had been fantastic. She knew my name and she was super friendly. Most other people would have just kept walking, but not Summer. No, she was too perfect. I had completely forgotten about her amidst the ACL tear and surgery, but in that car ride home I was reminded of how much love I had for this girl.

Before today, I was convinced that only a select number of people receive a miracle and the rest of us just get to listen to them tell their stories, hoping one day that we too would get their a miracle. I was a firm believer that I was just an ordinary kid who would never receive his miracle, but I was wrong.

Out of all the places and all the people in the world, my path collided with Summer's for the very first time in that parking lot in Ann Arbor.

That moment, the one so unexpected, was my miracle.

Chapter 20

The next few days were both a physical and emotional train wreck. At certain points my leg hurt so bad that there was nothing else to do but cry, which was very foreign to me. When I took medicine for the pain, it went away, only to be replaced by restlessness. I'm not one to ever consider killing myself, but if I did, it would be a result of being stir crazy. The feeling of wanting to move but knowing you can't is horrible. It was like living in a constant MRI scan.

Of course, my dad was not much help. I had to ask multiple times to even get him out of his office and do something for me, and after a while I became a burden to him. He did a good job talking to my doctors and making sure my road to recovery was on track, but I knew his only reason why.

One thing I learned in the week after my surgery was that I had taken my legs for granted. It was so hard to live with one functioning leg. I mean to freaking let my pee out of my bladder was a complicated and painful process that took almost ten minutes. Because the degree of difficulty that walking required, I basically lived on my living room couch. I had all my essentials within reach, so I didn't have to ask my dad to get me much except food. Most of my time was spent playing Xbox, where I completed a full season of Madden in career mode and won the Super bowl.

All the pain, discomfort, drugs, and boredom caused me to do a very stupid thing: I sent a message to Summer. The fact that I sent her a message wasn't the idiotic part; it was the way I did it and what I said. Any other high schooler knew how to talk to girls and would have sent a smooth, flirtatious message, but not me.

I went to her Instagram page and discovered part of the reason she had probably talked to me in that parking lot at the hospital. The "DT <3" and pictures with Davy on her page had been removed. They had broken up.

I had completely forgotten that Davy Trick was in the picture. The reason I had visited her Instagram page was not to check their relationship status, but to send Summer a DM, and find out why she actually talked to me. It wasn't normal for a girl like Summer to talk to guy like me, let alone be that friendly.

I clicked the "Direct Message" button and started tapping rapidly. I stopped, read over my message, and then deleted the entire thing. I tried again, only to completely delete it again. Everything had to be absolutely perfect. After many drafts, I finally came up with this:

"Hey, Summer. I was just wondering… what made you talk to me the other day? I know, dumb question, but, like, we had never talked before and you were so friendly!"

I hit the send button and regretted it right away.

"No, no, no, no, no," I moaned. *How could I have sent that?*

All she had done was show kindness toward me and now I was sending her Instagram direct messages asking her why.

I saw movement on the screen out of the corner of my eye and I turned my attention back to my phone. I thought she had seen the message or even replied already, but instead Instagram had sent me a notice that said, "SummerHarr1s has accepted your message request."

That's right; Summer didn't even follow me on Instagram. Perhaps she had only been nice because she felt like it was the right thing to do, since it was only us and our fathers with no one else around to make things awkward. People are always different when there are other people around they feel like they need to impress.

Slowly, my eyes began feeling heavy and my arms and legs followed soon after, feeling like they were being filled with lead. It felt really good, but I wasn't ready to sleep quite yet. Unfortunately, it wasn't my choice, and about five minutes later I fell asleep for the rest of the night.

When I woke up early the next morning, I couldn't fall back asleep. This was mainly for two reasons. The first, and most obvious, checking whether or not Summer had replied. If so, what did she say?

I felt around on my floor until I found my phone charger, and then pulled my phone up and pulled my phone back to my chest. I saw the black screen and knew there might have been a reply behind it. I closed my eyes, took a deep breath, and clicked the home button.

Nothing.

I had a few notifications, but none from Instagram. I opened the Instagram app to double check, but I didn't have any messages. She hadn't even seen it yet. Dozens of regrets flooded my mind and I felt even more stupid than before. This was my one chance and I was pretty sure that I had already screwed it up.

I then checked my messages from Shane, which was the second and least important reason I had woken up so early. After school, he was planning on coming over to see me for the first time in forever. I was so lonely that the thought of seeing someone else besides my dad felt like going to Disney World.

I confirmed my plans with Shane and started to text him about Summer, but stopped. I decided that I didn't want to tell anyone anything about Summer because I felt that if I did, it would automatically ruin everything from our small encounter.

I spent the rest of the day like every other, playing video games. When the clock hit half past three, I knew Shane would be over soon. He told me earlier to plan on four, so I anxiously awaited like a little kid would for a playdate.

I waited and waited. Pretty soon it was 4:30 in the afternoon and I hadn't heard from Shane. I decided to wait fifteen more minutes to say anything. When the time was up, I texted:

Me: Where u at?

Shane replied a few minutes later.

Shane: Oh, shoot, sorry bro. I went to Applebee's with Camilla. Does tomorrow work?

Just when I had started to think our friendship was completely back to normal, he wronged me in the worst possible way. I just had ACL surgery and he couldn't even take a half hour to come and visit me. Disappointment boiled inside of me and I texted him back right away.

Me: No, it's fine.

Shane: You sure, bro?

He didn't even feel guilty.

Me: Yep.

Shane: Cool. See you next week.

The rest of my day was pretty crappy. I was sick and tired of living like this and I couldn't wait to go back to school and finally see Summer. I didn't care how much my leg hurt. I needed to get out of that house. It wasn't my choice, however, on when I would be able to return to school. The doctor had sternly told me to wait at least a week.

I was playing versus the Patriots on Madden when my phone buzzed.

Shane, I assumed.

He better be apologizing or telling me he was on his way over. I paused the game, reached for my phone, and turned it on.

But, it wasn't from Shane. It was a message from Summer.

I read the first couple words, but then I laid my phone face down on my couch. I had to process this and prepare for whatever she said. I thought of every different and humiliating response she could have replied with, from Summer and Davy pulling a big prank on me, or her calling me a complete creep. Once I couldn't wait any longer to see her response, I slid my finger right across my phone screen and opened up my Instagram DM's.

My eyes took a couple of seconds to focus on what the words said. All my worries vanished as soon as I finished reading her reply.

"Sometimes when you find something... you just know:)"

Chapter 21

I spent the rest of my night trying to interpret what Summer meant. All I knew for sure, after hours of thinking, was that no matter what it was, it had to be something good. I wanted to talk to her for hours, share my deepest and darkest secrets, and tell her about my day and about Shane, and most importantly, about how much I love her.

But I didn't say any of that, playing it safe by responding with a simple smiley face. She read it almost right away, and didn't respond. I desired to talk with her more than anything, but I was content with leaving the conversation in a good spot.

My first day back could not come soon enough. I planned out exactly how I was going to walk into the classroom and what I would say to her. It had to be perfect.

In the meantime, I found an odd feeling of bliss. I knew that something amazing was waiting for me in Mrs. Wooten's classroom on Monday morning, and I could live with that. It was the best feeling in the world knowing something great was yet to come.

Eventually, Monday morning rolled around. It was my first time getting up this early for school in weeks and it actually felt pretty good. I had somehow managed to successfully clean my whole body in the shower the night before, and I was ready to go. I was ready to see Summer. I went through my normal morning routines like usual as if the three-week break had never happened. Now, though, everything took twice as long with my leg. I hadn't even thought about how people would react to my injury because I was too fixated on the whole Summer situation.

By 7:30 a.m., I was ready to leave. My dad would have to drive me to school for a while since I couldn't walk there anymore. I dreaded the car rides and the awkward silence that would dominate them, and it sure lived up to my expectations as not a single word was said until I got out of the car.

"See ya," he finally said.

"Bye," I closed the door and starting crutch-walking.

It was a lot harder than I thought. I had only ever used my crutches for a few steps around my house, but now having to walk long distances with them sucked. My armpits were already sore and it took me forever to walk a few feet.

Mostly everyone just stared at me or walked around me, but a few people asked what had happened. After a few times, I was already sick of explaining the story, but I knew it would come up again many times throughout the day.

"Hey! There he is!" some kid yelled to me from across the hall. I looked over trying to figure out who it was until they finally got closer. It was Shane, and he looked completely different. He'd cut his long hair so that he had a haircut similar to mine, short on the sides with a comb over on the top.

"Hey," I said, still upset. "What's with the hair?"

"Camilla convinced me!" he chuckled. This wasn't Shane, changing his freaking hairstyle for a girl he'd never see again after more four months.

I rolled my eyes and snorted, "Really, dude?"

"Uh," his smile faded. "Is there a problem?"

I could have said no, faked being fine, and we would have gone on with our lives. But I'm not that type of person. If someone has mistreated me or done something wrong, I let them know about it.

"Yeah, Shane, there is," I restabled myself on my crutches.

"Oh, yeah?" he took a step closer. Surely he wasn't threatening me, the kid who was one week post knee surgery.

I stood my ground. "You're different, man. You've changed."

"You've gotta be kidding, bro," he laughed defensively. "Of course I've changed. I've got a girlfriend! You've just got your foot up your butt now that I can't spend every minute worrying about your problems."

"So you justify everything you've done? You don't feel guilt for anything?"

"WHAT HAVE I DONE, URIAH?" he yelled out with confusion.

"Hmm, well for starters, you can't even take your precious time away from Camilla to come see your best friend who JUST HAD KNEE SURGERY! What else, oh yeah, you've blown me off for lunch every day, leaving me to sit by myself EVERY SINGLE DAY."

I could feel my hands becoming sweaty on the crutch handles.

"And what about a few weeks ago when you screwed up your face? Who was the first person you called? And, who was the first person that came?" he hissed.

"You brought Camilla and I had never even met her before. You know how awkward that was? I thought we'd always have each other's back, but you let me down, dude."

"You know what," he couldn't even refute everything I had just said. "I'm not putting up with you anymore. Look, I'm sorry you got your leg hurt and all, but you are just an unappreciative loser who only cares about himself."

If I wouldn't have been on crutches I'm certain I would have shoved him. I stared at him with my nostrils flaring, and he stared right back with the same intensity.

After a few seconds, I said, "Fine then, go and choose your ugly foreign exchange girlfriend over your best friend. When she's gone forever in a few months, don't even think you can try being my friend again."

I had never seen Shane that mad in our whole friendship and I was certain he was going to shove, kick or punch me. But then he backed off and started walking backwards.

"You're lucky you're on crutches, you twig. Better watch out for yourself after you can walk again."

He turned and walked away. Complete strangers. I never would have imagined him saying those words to me.

After Shane was out of sight, I started walking to my first hour, which was algebra 2 for the new semester. Math was always my worst subject and I hated it with a passion, but today, for an obvious reason, I was stoked about math.

Almost everyone I passed stared at me and at first my thought was that somehow my argument with Shane had spread around the school and I was the one tagged as the bad guy.

To my relief, I remembered that it was because of my crutches. *Surely no one had overheard, had they?* When I got to the stairs that would bring me to my first hour, I remembered the elevator would be my best friend for the next couple months.

Exhausted already, I made my way to the elevator and pressed the button. A few seconds later, it beeped and the door opened. A few ghetto kids, who were clearly too lazy to use the stairs, walked out. They cleared into the hallway and I got in for the appropriate reason. My school only had two floors so it didn't take long to find the correct button. The elevator alerted with a ding and then proceeded to close. The ride was short and sweet and when the door opened again, I stepped out in pursuit of my class. While making sure to look out for Shane, I completely forgot about Camilla. She was walking on the opposite side of the hallway in my direction.

"Oh my goodness, Ooreeah," she butchered my name. "What happened?"

"Oh, um," she caught me off guard. I guess she didn't know about my argument with Shane yet, though it had only happened a few minutes ago. "I tore my ACL."

"A. C. L.?"

"It's a muscle in my leg," I had to be quick. "Listen, I gotta get to class, Camilla!"

"Okay, um," she seemed to be searching the dictionary in her brain. "Be well!"

I had dodged a bullet there. With the way Shane was always glued to her hip, he was bound to be in the area at any second. Everything would have been a hundred times worse if he saw me with his girlfriend. I'm not sure if I meant it when I told him to not come crawling back when she goes back home, but I knew I would just have to see how things played out.

That wasn't my main concern now, though. Whatever awaited in class C-1002 was. I had felt so confident when conversations with Summer were just thoughts in my head, but in just a few seconds it would be happening for real. I started feeling sick and pondered whether or not I should go to the bathroom, but the feeling went away quickly. It was 7:54, and everyone would be crowding the halls in a minute. I couldn't afford to get caught up in any big crowds with my leg, so I had no choice but to knock on the door.

Mrs. Wooten walked over and opened the door.

"Oh my, you poor thing!" she said after seeing my leg.

"Heh, thanks," I said in a very awkward way.

How was I ever going to be normal around Summer if I was already fumbling for words around my 60-year-old teacher? It had been so easy the first time, when it was unexpected. The human mind, while being the basis for everything we do, can also be very destructive. Overthinking is the greatest example.

"Well, I'll get out of way!" she said, moving to open up as much space in the doorway for me as possible. I gingerly walked in and scanned the room. Summer wasn't in class yet, which was normal. What senior got to class five minutes early?

In fact, only a couple of kids were in the room. Ester, a short redhead who took school very seriously and had no personality, was sitting in the very front row. Behind her sat a kid named Will, who seemed pretty cool but I had never talked to him, which I really regretted now. The only friend I had ever really needed was Shane, but now that he was out of the equation, I had no one.

I took a seat in the very back of the room and laid my crutches on the ground. The bell signaling first hour rang and I waited.

Slowly, the class filled up with students. Most of them were sophomores, like me, but there was a select amount of juniors and seniors, all of whom were there, except Summer.

The bell was about to ring again and she hadn't arrived at class yet. Like it always does, my mind started overthinking and speculating why she wasn't there.

Calm down, I told myself. *She will come.*

But then the clock hit 8 a.m. and that meant one of two things, Summer either wasn't in this class anymore or she was just late. I prayed it would be the latter and that I would hear a knock on the door any minute.

Mrs. Wooten started welcoming the class to a brand new day and reviewed what they had been working on last week, but I wasn't listening. Even though I should have been, as I missed an entire week. But, I couldn't get my mind off where Summer could be. I had been looking forward to this moment for days now. I thought about sending her another message on Instagram, but that would be way too assertive.

I wish she would just come already; it's killing me.

Then suddenly, like I secretly had a genie granting me wishes, I heard a knock on the door. My heart stopped, as well as Mrs. Wooten's teaching about sin, cosine, and tangent.

She walked over and opened the door. Every head turned to see who it was, especially mine.

Instead of Summer, it was just some random girl who was always late to class.

"You're not having a good start to the semester, Ms. Ramirez," my teacher said, irritated as she updated the attendance chart.

My hopes of Summer showing up were now even lower than before. Maybe she was just sick or not at school for some reason. I tried to stop thinking about it as I needed to catch up on my algebra.

The last fifteen minutes of class were always homework and catch-up time. Mrs. Wooten was sitting next to me going through all the notes, lessons, and homework from the past week. Overwhelmed, I didn't even hear the knock on the door. I stared at a worksheet trying to figure out what sin divided by cos equals when a girl walked up to my table. I looked up, at first confused, then realized it was Summer. I stared at her momentarily, unsure why she was just standing right next to our table, when I noticed the late slip she had for Mrs. Wooten.

"Oh, hi, Summer!" she took the red slip. "We are just doing homework time right now, feel free to take a seat and I'll get you the notes."

Our eyes met and she smiled. It was a simple gesture, a lot different than last week, but it still warmed my entire body. She then began searching the room for an open seat.

Please get up, Mrs. Wooten. Please get up, I silently pleaded. But she didn't, so Summer took a seat two chairs over from me. Almost right as she sat down, Mrs. Wooten got up because, you know, things never seemed to go my way. Annoyed, I tried to act normal while finishing up my notes.

The bell rang signaling the end of first hour and I started packing up my stuff. I put all my weight on the table and pushed myself up, only to realize I had forgotten my crutches. I had started to sit down again when Summer stopped me.

"I got it!" she smiled and picked them up for me. She was still as nice as she had been last week, just less enthusiastic. She must not have been a morning person, I concluded.

"Thanks so much," I smiled back. "I got worried when you weren't here."

"Rough morning," she giggled and pointed to her face. "As you can probably tell."

"No, I couldn't," I found myself whispering. "You look great."

The room around us was dead silent, but it wasn't awkward. Summer had a way of making my nerves disappear. I truly felt like myself around her. And yet, we'd spoken only a couple short times. What would happen if we really got to know each other? If we had late night phone calls and lengthy dinner discussions? How amazing would I feel then?

A few seconds later, she interrupted the silence and said, "Hey, I gotta go to my next class, but I'll see you tomorrow? I'll actually get here on time and I can sit by you."

"Sounds great," I nodded my head.

I walked through the door as she kindly held it open for me, and then we separated in different directions.

Chapter 22

No matter how hard you try, things will never happen the way you imagine them to. For example, how Summer and I became friends. I had always pictured some dudes being douches to her and me coming in to save the day, causing her to realize how great I was and befriend me. But things *don't* work out how you expect and the way Summer and I became friends is Example A.

I would have never seen Summer in Ann Arbor if it weren't for my race. I pleaded with my dad to let me skip this race, but if I had won that argument, we never would have crossed paths. But I did go to the race, and I won the qualifier. But, what if I hadn't? I would have never torn my ACL and had to have surgery, eventually leading me to meet Summer that very day. Even the little details, such as stopping to buy bottled water at the hospital cafeteria before leaving, affected the timing of our fateful meeting. Destiny is a very cliché word, but God was watching out for me, even if it meant experiencing the most pain I had ever felt in my life.

Yet, I was still confused. Why was she all of a sudden so nice to me? I mean, she wasn't exactly mean before, but the change in her from my encounter with Davy to seeing her in the parking lot at the hospital was so drastic. She had even been friendly to me in class when other people were around, proving she genuinely meant it.

This question plagued me all day, and the constant reminder that I had just lost my best friend didn't help at all. When I had the chance, I would ask her in the morning.

I felt the urge to text Shane and tell him about Summer, but I remembered what had happened that morning. After all, I had told him not come crawling back. How hypocritical would I be if I did just that?

That night, I was playing more Xbox after catching up on all my schoolwork. I was en route to my third consecutive Super Bowl with the Lions when I heard my dad's office door open and him walk out. His hair was a mess and he looked super stressed.

"Hey," he sighed.

"Hi," I replied keeping my eyes glued to the screen.

"How's your little situation going?"

"What?" I paused.

How did he know my crush on Summer?

"Uh, your leg?" he said rather snotty.

"Oh, um," I paused the game. "It's doing okay. It feels better and better every day."

"Well, good. It sucks you won't be able to run for so long."

"I was thinking, maybe I could quit running, like you," I tried to not sound like a jerk.

"No. That was my biggest regret. Well, one of them. Your knee will actually be stronger after this. You have lots of potential in those skinny legs yet."

I could have argued with him about it but there was no point, plus I didn't feel like getting slapped. This whole thing with Summer made me feel like a man, but that would be stripped away with a single slap from my father's large hand.

I woke up that next morning with even more energy and excitement than the day before. Twenty-four hours earlier I was shaking and uneasy, but that was all gone now. I had found a confidence in myself like never before.

The only hiccup to my morning was seeing Shane in the hallway. We both saw each other as we passed in the art wing, but he looked through me like I was invisible and just kept walking. I was definitely furiated with him, but it still felt really weird. For such a long time, we had been best friends who never stopped talking when around each other.

But I couldn't let that ruin my spirits. I had more important things to focus on. Mrs. Wooten was holding open the door for her first-hour students, and she greeted me with a gentle head nod. I sat in the same place as yesterday, even though there was not an assigned seating chart.

Unlike yesterday, Summer was the first person to come into the room after I had sat down. She appeared to be on a mission, one that wasn't complete until she found her seat next to mine.

"Hi!" she sighed, sitting down.

"Hey, what's up?" I asked, not knowing what else to say.

The room was really filling in now. It was hard to ignore the people who stared at the rarity of a senior and sophomore sitting next to each other, but I really didn't care. Everything I had wished for over the past few months was now sitting right beside me. I was going to enjoy it. I just had to make sure I said and did the right things so not to come across the wrong way. After all, I had somehow gotten to this point, I couldn't blow it now.

"Can I borrow the notes from yesterday?" she asked casually. I couldn't tell if the gut-wrenching feeling I had was mutual or not.

"Yeah, no problem," I said as I pulled out my folder and handed her a couple papers.

"Oh, my gosh, Uriah!" she frightened me. "Why are you shaking?"

I looked down at my hand, which was twitching rather abnormally. I knew, of course, the source came from nerves, but I couldn't let her know that. I didn't think she knew that I had a crush on her, so I came up with the best excuse possible in the spare of the moment.

"Oh, uh, it's a side effect from this medicine I'm taking for my leg," I was confident with my lie.

"Oh, okay," she believed it, or at least seemed to. "How's your leg, anyway?"

"It's good, still hurts a lot though sometimes."

"Can I admit something?"

"Yes?"

"I really wanna see what your leg looks like," she blushed. "Like, is it bruised? What do the stitches look like? Doctorish stuff like that has always fascinated me."

"It's nothing special," I started, but realized this was my chance. "Maybe you could see it though, if we ever hung out or something."

She had an expression in her face that was really hard to interpret. She either felt badly for giving me the wrong impression, or she was super excited and just didn't know what to say. My stomach dropped as I waited for a response. Her face changed expressions what seemed like a half dozen times; my heart rate getting quicker with each one.

"Yeah," she whispered in a way that sent goosebumps across my entire body. "That would be great."

Chapter 23

It was a week and a half before Summer and I actually hung out, and while uneventful, it was some of the best days of my life. Yes, I was no longer friends with Shane, but I found out it was rather relaxing not having to fight with Camilla over his time and attention.

My leg was getting better with every passing day and on top of that, it was very hard to have a bad day when my days started out by sitting next to Summer in math class. We weren't able to have the long conversations I so eagerly craved, but the small talk and friendship we began to develop was priceless.

I wish I could say our first two weeks of getting to know each other was an epic love story, you know, like Ron Weasley and Hermione Granger, but like I've always said, most of the time you don't get to choose how things work out. Summer and I talked every single day about little stuff that had no significant meaning except that is made us happy. Some days we would gossip about teachers and other days we would discuss our favorite television shows. It was a daily thing, except for mornings when I had to miss class for my leg therapy.

Eventually, the classroom sessions with Summer felt redundant, so it was refreshing to know that Friday night Summer and I were planning on going out to eat at Red Robin.

When the morning bell rang, Summer asked, "Pick you up at, like, seven?"

"Yeah, sounds good."

I was a little embarrassed that I hadn't gotten my license yet. I was already 16, but I was too lazy to take driver's education.

"See you then," she tilted her head and smiled, then walked out of the room as I packed my stuff up.

I'm not gonna lie; it felt like we were nothing more than just really close friends, but it really didn't matter. All I cared about was being with her because when in her presence, I found happiness that I had once believed was unreachable.

The rest of the day went by really, really slowly. Time is a very weird concept to me, five minutes can seem like a blink of the eye when you have to get up for school in the morning, but it feels like an eternity when you're stuck in a boring class.

I was so ecstatic to hang out with Summer that as soon as I got home I started planning out when I needed to start getting ready. I decided that I would shower around 6 p.m. and then hopefully by the time I got my leg back in my brace, I would have time to pick out the best outfit to wear.

When all was said and done, I stood in front of my bathroom mirror wearing an Andre Drummond jersey with a grey Nike sweatshirt underneath. It took me a long time to decide what to wear for a shirt, but I couldn't say the same for pants, as I chose the first khakis I saw in my closet. No style of pants looked better than any other when a giant knee brace dominated most of my left leg.

It was almost time for Summer to pick me up and it hadn't even cross my mind how I would pay. I knew I had to pay for Summer's food, as well as mine, but all I had was six dollars in my wallet and five quarters on my desk. I walked downstairs to find my dad and he was eating cereal while watching the news.

My dad was loaded, but he rarely gave me money to do anything. It was yet another downside to having a father that only liked you when you were winning track races. The next nine months of my life would be hell when I was around him because the doctors had told me absolutely no running until my recovery was complete.

"Hey, dad, I'm going out with a friend to Red Robin. Do you think I could have some money?" I asked with unrealistic high hopes.

"Don't you have any money left from that twenty I gave you at Christmas?" he turned and gave me a dirty look.

"I only have six dollars left."

"Well, there you go. Just get something cheap then. Shane can pay for himself."

"But, I have to pay for both of us tonight."

It would be best if he didn't know I was going with a girl.

"Shane's parents have money. He can pay for himself," my dad stood firm with his decision.

"No, you see Red Robin can get expensive so we decided to alternate who pays when we go," I tried to sound convincing.

"Well, that's just a stupid idea. I need to teach you how to manage money better," he grunted.

After ignoring his last comment for a few seconds, I asked again, "Sooooooo?"

He let out a huge sigh. "Fine. There's a twenty in my wallet, but no more! Don't make this a habit."

"Awesome. Thanks!" I left the room without giving him time to change his mind.

I walked into the kitchen and found his wallet, which was filled with twenties, fifties, and even hundreds. I could have stolen a twenty and I'm pretty sure my dad would have never noticed. As I transferred the bill from his wallet to mine, I felt the vibration of a text message against my leg. It was, as expected, a message from Summer.

Summer: Here :)

I picked up my resting crutch and went as fast as I could so I didn't make her wait too long. I walked out of my house without saying goodbye to my dad and made my way carefully to Summer's car. I could hear the bass vibrating from inside the car, but as soon as I made my way to the door, it stopped. Summer graciously pushed open the passenger's side door so I could get inside the car, which proved to be a bit of a struggle. It was super embarrassing, but I felt better after she laughed at my sarcastic comment, "That went well!"

Her car was unexpectedly clean to belong to a teenager girl. It smelled of red raspberries from the air freshener hanging from her mirror. She told me I could put my crutches in the back seat, so I carefully placed them one at a time on her perfect, leather seats.

"Off to Red Robin!" she said as she put her car in reverse. Instead of saying anything, I caught myself just smiling at her. She had the type of beauty that captivates you.

"So is Red Robin your favorite restaurant?" she asked me after I typed the address in to her Google Maps.

"Oh, it's amazing! My favorite restaurant by far!" I exclaimed.

"Amazing? I'll be the judge of that!" she smirked.

"Wait," I could feel myself become more and more comfortable with Summer. "You've never actually tried Red Robin?"

"Nope, never," she shook her head.

"WHO RAISED YOU?!" I purposely dramatized each word to be funny.

"Hey! Give me a break!" she laughed, thankfully.

"I feel bad!" I said in a more apologetic tone. "We could have gone somewhere you wanted to. It would have been no problem."

I had to do everything I could to be as nice as possible. That was my biggest problem with making friends; I came off as a mean person to a lot of people, even though I'm not. It's just my sarcastic personality.

"No, no, I want to go to Red Robin. I need to try new things."

"Is that why you are hanging out with me?" I winked.

Note to self: Never wink like that again.

"What do you mean!?"

"Well, you were just dating Davy a few weeks ago and now you are hanging out with a sophomore!"

Summer had never formally told me that she and Davy broke up, but she knew that I knew and we were fine leaving it at that.

"Oh, don't even get me started. I will tell you all about that situation when we get there," she dodged my initial questions.

"Can't wait," I chuckled as she came to a stop at a red light.

Summer and I walked into the restaurant, and the smell of fries and burgers infiltrated our nostrils. The bar area was way too loud, so we took the booth that was the farthest away. Right after we sat down, a large lady named Ronda came over and asked what we wanted to drink. We both ordered waters and started looking over the menu.

"What should I get?" she asked me. It was a lot of pressure. Whatever she ordered needed to be perfect.

"Hmmmm," I scanned the menu I had practically memorized. "You can't go wrong with the chicken tenders and fries. It's what I always get. It's legit!"

"Maybe… maybe," she shook her head, still looking at the menu.

A few minutes later, Ronda came back with our waters and asked if we were ready to order. I gestured to Summer and she started ordering.

"I'll take the chicken tenders and fries," she said as she folded her menu.

"Any dipping sauce?"

"Um, ranch?"

"And for you?" Ronda turned to me.

"I'll take the exact same thing!" I closed my menu and gave them both to her.

'I'll get those right in. You guys let me know if you need anything," Ronda said and walked off.

Summer and I simultaneously turned our heads from Ronda and made eye contact.

"So," I dragged on for a couple seconds. "It's hard really getting to know someone in math class. Tell me about yourself."

"You can't just put me on the spot like that!" I could see her blushing. I felt bad for embarrassing her.

"Sorry!" I jokingly mocked and took a sip of my water.

"If it's so easy, then how about you answer every question I do?" she said with a "take that!" expression.

"You're on!"

"Okay, okay," she said. "What first?"

My mind went blank. It was really hard to think of good questions that weren't something basic like favorite food or color. Without realizing I would have to answer my own question, I blurted out, "Tell me about your family!"

I instantly saw her happy expression shift into a scared, nervous one. I knew of her dad, and he was pretty cool, but I didn't know anything else about her family.

"Um... you first!"

I quickly thought about what I'd say, but it'd really be a buzzkill. If the first thing I told her about myself was that my mom had been murdered and my dad actually hated me, it wouldn't make for good conversation.

"Let's skip family for now," I suggested and she agreed.

This was not going well. I was sitting across the table from the girl of my dreams and I somehow couldn't come up with anything interesting to talk about. I knew there was something there. I just couldn't quite grasp ahold of it.

"Uh, so do you like algebra?" I desperately asked.

"What? Oh, well, it's okay. I do really good in the class but it's not exactly fun."

I nodded my head and searched every section of my brain for the question I wanted to ask.

Come on think! I pleaded with my hippocampus.

Then all of a sudden, it finally came back to me, the question I had been longing to hear the answer to.

"So, I have a question for you," I folded my hands together.

"Shoot it," she looked relaxed now, like no question could phase her.

"What exactly did you mean when you said 'Sometimes you just find something and you just know?' Like, why me? Why were you so nice to someone you barely knew?"

"Uriah Peterson!" she scowled at me, but with a smile. "Are you trying to convince me to not to have a thing for you anymore?"

"No, no, no!" I stuttered trying not to freak out concerning what she had just mentioned about having a thing for me. "I'm just curious, because you know that like... never happens."

She seemed to mentally prepare her response, then finally spoke, "Listen, Uriah, that morning I was in a bad place. When I woke up, I asked God to send me a sign.

Something to lift my spirits a little bit, you know? And then, hours away from the comfort of my home, there you were in that parking lot. I don't think it was any coincidence that it was the sophomore I couldn't stop thinking about."

There was my explanation. Not only was she my miracle, but I was also hers.

Trying to keep my emotions from exploding with happiness, I asked a follow-up question, "Why couldn't you stop thinking about me?"

"I'm so sorry, Uriah, about that one day," she looked truly heartbroken. "Davy was such a jerk to you and Shane and I didn't do a thing about it."

"No!" I tried convincing her it was okay. "Look, that's in the past and you broke up with him so it doesn't really matter. Is that why you broke up with him?"

"No, well, I mean in the broad scheme of things I guess it contributed, but we didn't officially break up until after the holidays," she was obviously still traumatized from that bastard.

"I hate him so much," I said in disgust. "What made you officially end things?"

"The day after New Year's I found out that I got accepted into my dream college, NC State," she started.

I could see where this was going.

"When I told him, he didn't even congratulate me. He just asked how long we'd be able to date. I was so angry at him. This was life changing and it was clear that all he wanted was more time to try and get me in bed with him. I left his house that night bawling my eyes out, not because I had broken up with him, but because that was one of the most hurtful things anyone had ever said to me."

I could see all the emotions flooding her red face. I had to do something quickly, something to cheer her up.

"Well, he doesn't matter. I am super proud of you for following your dreams and I won't stop being your friend because you are going to be leaving for college!" I said, even though the thought killed me.

"Uriah," she looked me straight in the eye. "You don't know how much that actually means to me."

"Wanna hear the nickname I call him?" I asked, enlightening the mood.

"And what is that?" she half-smiled.

It was working.

"Instead of calling him Davy Trick, I call him Davy Prick."

She burst out laughing, even though the nickname was really only kind of funny.

"I have never thought about that! Prick doesn't even begin to describe the way he treated me," she was more angry than sad now.

"Examples? Come on, let it all out," I gestured with my hand.

"Okay, well... Oh! Well, one time when we first started dating and I hadn't seen his terrible side yet, I asked him if we could go to this love bridge, where you put love locks with your names on them and stuff, and he called it gay and told me he would never go to something that sappy. I've wanted to do something like that for years. It's on my bucket list, but he wouldn't do it."

"Does he know you should never say something like that to a girl?" I exaggerated my disbelief at how much of a jerk he was.

"Apparently not!"

"You loved him?" I asked.

"No."

Finally, after countless stories about the evilness of Davy, Ronda brought us our food.

"Is there anything else I can get for you two?" Ronda asked as we inhaled the aroma of the freshly-cooked food.

"I think we are fine!" Summer smiled with all thirty-two perfect teeth.

I went to grab for a chicken strip, but was stopped by Summer, who was taking a picture of me.

After she got her picture, I took a bite and asked, "Had to get it for the Snap?"

"Of course!" she flirted back. "Oh my gosh, we aren't even Snapchat friends!"

"Well, add me!"

"What's your username?"

"Don't judge me, I made this back when I was like thirteen... It's obiwan2442."

She mocked me about my username as we ate our food. Even after we finished eating, I had no plans on leaving any time soon. Our conversation was too amazing.

As she explained why Lil Uzi Vert was better than Lil Yachty, I tried to muster up something from our previous dialogue that we could talk about. It had been so hard earlier, but it was really easy now.

"So, you said earlier that you prayed to God. Was that just a figure of speech or are you a legit Christian?"

Right away she answered, "I'm a Christian, for sure. You?"

"Yes, kind of," I replied.

"What do you mean?" she asked me.

"I believe and everything, it's just..." I was at a loss for words. She stared at me, patiently waiting for me to explain.

"Here's a good analogy. The parable of the farmer spreading seeds. I'm like the seed that gets planted in the rocky soil. I want to be a Christian, but I just don't have deep enough roots to produce a good harvest," I said.

"You seem to know the Bible well. Do you go to church?"

"No. I mean, I did a few times with my grandparents when they were alive, but I haven't in years."

"I think that is probably your biggest problem. You should come with me sometime!"

I started to accept her offer, but Ronda came by with the check. Summer and I both grabbed for it. Our hands touched and a warm sensation flowed throughout my chest and down to my arms and legs. I had never touched her before, but now that I had, I never wanted our skin to separate.

"Move your hand. My dad is rich," she said, not as mesmerized as I was.

I came back to reality, and replied, "So is mine, and *I'm* the guy."

"You make a valid argument. Thank you!" she smiled and her nose crinkled in the most adorable way.

I put the twenty-dollar bill with the $16.59 check, and Ronda came back to pick it up. I told her I didn't need change back, so she thanked me and told us have a good night.

While Summer and I did not verbally communicate it to each other, it was evident that we both wanted to stay and keep talking. The night had gotten off to an awkward beginning, but now we couldn't shut up. We talked about so much that by the end of the night we were debating ridiculous topics, like which was better, Target or Meijer.

"You are crazy if you think Meijer is better than Target!" she was gasping for air from laughing too hard.

"Meijer has better quality products and is way cheaper!"

"But, Meijer is a grocery store. Target has everything!"

We laughed through the rest of the conversation then I pulled out my phone for the first time since we had gotten to the restaurant.

"Holy crap, it's 9:45 already!"

She looked at my phone to make sure I wasn't joking.

"Ready to leave?" she asked.

"Let's go," I said putting my coat on and picking up my crutches.

It took a few minutes for the car to warm up and when it finally became a bearable temperature, she put the car in reverse and drove off. I was really bummed that the night was ending, but I was hopeful that Summer was having as good of a time as me and would want to hang out again soon.

When she pulled into my driveway, I unclicked my seatbelt. I looked over at her and she looked right back at me. I wanted to kiss her, really badly. It was the middle of winter and yet her lips had no cracks; they were completely perfect, completely ready to be kissed. For the first time all night, silence wasn't a bad thing.

I had never felt an urge like this in my entire life. Everything I ever wanted and ever would want was right in front of me. I may still be a teenage boy, but this was not a feeling of lust. It was a strong attraction.

I looked into Summer's eyes and knew she wanted to kiss me too. It was happening. There was no doubt about it. I leaned in at a very slow pace and I couldn't quite tell, but I think she did too.

But then, we simultaneously stopped. It was not the right time. It killed me a little inside, but the choice felt right. Whatever we had going was too great to waste our first kiss in her car, in my driveway.

"You know what I realized?" she spoke for the first time in minutes.

"What's that?" I asked.

"You never showed me your leg! We had a deal!"

"We never specified when!" I teased her and opened the car door. "I guess you'll just have to hang out with me again if you really want to see it."

"Sounds like a date," she said gently.

A date.

"Bye, Summer."

"Bye, Uriah."

Chapter 24

I finally understood what Shane meant when he said things change when you get a girlfriend. Even though it would be exactly a week until Summer and I hung out again, I yearned to spend every minute of every day with her. Still, that didn't excuse the fact that he treated me the way he did. Shane had completely cut me off, which included blocking me on Facebook, Snapchat, and Instagram. When I told Summer about the whole situation, I regretted doing so as she tried to persuade me to apologize.

"Me? Apologize?" I couldn't believe what I hearing. "He should be the one begging me to be his friend again!"

"I know, Uriah," she said pulling out our homework from the previous night. "But life is short, and you will regret it if your friendship with him is never rekindled."

She had a point, but I was way too stubborn to admit it.

"I'll give it some more time. Who knows, maybe he and Camilla will break up soon."

Mrs. Wooten started a lesson so Summer and I could not continue the conversation any longer. After a long and boring lesson about quadratics, it was homework time. But our homework was soon forgotten and we found ourselves discussing Detroit sports teams instead. I did most of the talking, but she did know a little bit about the teams.

We finally shifted our focus and finished our homework early enough that we had time to pack our stuff up and wait for the bell to ring. At 9 a.m., the bell rang and we walked out to the halls. Yes, I actually WALKED.

It had been about a month since my surgery and after lots of therapy and leg care, my doctor told me I could walk without crutches as long as I kept my leg brace on. It was still difficult to walk while wearing the brace, but it was loads easier than having to use crutches everywhere I went.

Summer walked at a very slow pace so I could keep up as we headed toward the table where we always sat and talked after first hour. Our relationship was now at the level of us meeting up after every class.

We were almost to the table when we saw him--the very last person in the entire world that I would want to see. It was Davy and he was walking our way. I would have spent two more weeks on crutches just to have it be anyone else, even Shane!

I looked over at Summer with an anxious expression. Without looking back at me, she said, "Just ignore whatever he says and do not try to be a hero, promise?"

I acted like I had planned on doing something, but then agreed not to for Summer. In reality, there was no chance I was going to start anything with Davy. He was at least twice my size AND I still had a very fragile leg.

I watched Davy the whole way. Once he passed us, he turned around backwards, staring right at us.

Oh, how the tides had turned. A couple months ago this exact situation in this exact same hallway had occurred, but now Summer was walking alongside me instead of Davy. He was probably thinking about that same thing because out of anger or jealousy, or who knows what, Davy yelled out to me, "Sloppy seconds!"

Everyone in the hall turned their heads toward Summer and me. Some started laughing, some were shocked that we were together, and some didn't really care and kept going on about their business.

The comment didn't bother me at all. It was actually kind of satisfying to see him jealous. Summer was perfect and I knew he didn't really mean "sloppy seconds." He was just obviously upset that he lost her to me.

But the comment really bothered Summer. She thought everyone viewed her as another one of Davy's "used up" victims when in reality, she had done absolutely NOTHING with Davy Prick. Just like she had done nothing to upset him, yet he still treated her that way. There are many good people in this world, but sadly there are just as many evil ones.

I looked at her as we kept walking and said, "Screw him. He knows that's not true."

Her face had changed to a peach-colored red from embarrassment.

"I know. Life just sucks sometimes," she said really casually.

We both tried to ignore the looks we got from everyone regarding what had just happened, but it was almost impossible to ignore the look on Shane's face. He walked by with Camilla, smirking at me. I didn't see him in the hallway with Davy, but I know he had to have seen what happened. But he did nothing, so much unlike the last encounter I had with Davy. The look he gave me--a look of mockery and amusement--made it clear that our friendship was over. Pathetic really, considering it was over a foreign exchange student. I wondered what he thought about my relationship with Summer. He was the only person on this Earth that knew of my love for her, and now we were dating. Did he simply not care? Or, deep down was he a little happy for me? While I wished I knew the answer to that question, the look he gave me implied that we were now strangers.

Summer and I stopped and took a seat our usual table.

"Did you see Shane?" she asked me, obviously trying to avoid any conversation about Davy.

"Yeah, it felt weird. Like he was supposed to be there and have my back again. But things change, I guess."

"They do and it sucks sometimes."

"Change sucks every time!" I stared at the fake-wooden table.

"Does not!" she proclaimed.

"Like when?" I asked.

"Two months ago I was dating Davy, the most selfish, rude, and ugly guy that I can think of," she grabbed my right hand. "And now, here I am with the sweetest, funniest, and most handsome boyfriend ever. If you ask me, that's one of the best changes I could have ever asked for."

Chapter 25

"Wait, wait, wait! So, you're telling me he wet the bed until he was thirteen years old?" I was dying with laughter over what Summer had just told me.

"Yes, no joke! He had to wear adult diapers!" Summer shared from across the booth. She was laughing as hysterically as me.

"How come you haven't used that against him?" I wiped the tears from my face.

"I don't know, I would feel bad," she controlled her laugh.

We were in Red Robin again, sitting in the exact same booth as before. We had both ordered the chicken tenders and fries, and Summer was telling me embarrassing stuff about Davy that no one else knew.

"Okay, okay, enough about him. Let's talk about something different," she said, either because she was sick of talking about him or because she had run out of stories, maybe both.

"You know who I feel bad for?" I asked looking across the restaurant.

"Who's that?" she asked as she took a sip of water.

"Ronda," who was taking the order of another table. "I mean she gets paid like three dollars an hour, gets terrible tips, and has to clean up after everybody."

"Don't forget the fact that she's stuck here every Friday night," Summer added.

"I could never do it," I shook my head.

"Have you ever had a job before?" she asked me.

"No, and I don't plan to anytime soon."

"Me neither. No point when I'm going to college..." she trailed off at the end.

I tried to ignore the fact that sometime in August, Summer was going to board a plane and fly to a place where she would live hundreds of miles away from me. I knew it would be tough, but that was another problem for another time.

"What do you wanna do for Valentine's Day?" she changed the conversation.

Valentine's Day.

It was next week and I hadn't even started thinking about what I was going to do for Summer.

"Let's see a movie!" I suggested even though I had no intentions of actually seeing a movie. I had to do something big, something bold. Of course, seeing a movie would have been perfectly fine, but that was too boring. I could do way better than that. This is Summer we are talking about!

"Okay!" she looked perfectly contempt with a movie.

"What do you want to see?" I asked.

"It doesn't matter to me," Summer said. "But whatever you do, no big red heart balloons or teddy bears that I'll have to carry around all day at school. I cringe so hard when I see that."

"Agreed!" I laughed.

All I knew was that I wanted to do something out of the ordinary, but I had no idea what it would be yet. I spent the rest of our date silently trying to muster up the perfect night, and I even looked up some ideas on my phone when she went to the bathroom, but every single one was stupid.

When she dropped me off at my house, a good idea was still absent from my brain and I had become extremely worried. I was always good at coming up with ideas, but now my mind was completely blank. I needed to decide on my game plan quickly. Valentine's Day wasn't that far away and surely it would take some time to prepare for whatever I chose to do. I fell asleep that night still trying to come up with an idea, but failed. But then, in the middle of the night, I woke up, and I don't know how or why, but I knew exactly what I would do for Summer on Valentine's Day.

Chapter 26

I stood in front of the closed door that led down to my basement, trying to brave the thought of whatever stood behind it. I had not been in the basement for years now. It always scared me as a child and I never really grew out of it. I wasn't scared of imaginary monsters or ghosts, but the thought of all my mother's belongings down there always sent shivers down my spine. After she died, my dad couldn't handle going through all her stuff so he just kept it in the basement, where it has sat for fifteen years.

The last memory I have of being in the basement was when I was just a small child, curious to learn more about my mom. I began going through a bunch of photos and, at the time, they freaked me out so much because I didn't even recognize her. I ran up the stairs screaming and crying. After that, I always stayed far away from that door, fearing that if I even got too close, those pictures would hauntingly come flying out at me.

Even though I swore to myself I would never enter that basement again, I knew it was necessary to create the perfect Valentine's Day gift for Summer. I lifted my hand and twisted the cold, brass handle. The stiffness the door possessed told me it indeed had not been opened in years. After a hard yank, the door came unstuck from the door frame and opened.

I peered down the stairs into complete darkness and started doubting whether or not I wanted to do this.

No, not ready, I came to a decision.

I turned around and started walking away, but then I stopped.

I have to do this. I can't ruin such a good idea by being a chicken.

The first thing I had to do was find a light; there was no way I would walk down those stairs in the dark. I used my phone's flashlight app to find the light switch that was directly to my right. When I flicked the switch up, it took a few seconds for the light to finally flicker on, revealing the outdated carpeted stairs.

Even with my bad leg, I walked slower than I should have. I could see the light switch for the rest of the basement at the bottom of the stairs, and I was not looking forward to what I so vaguely remembered from my childhood. From two or three steps away, I reached over and grazed the switch just enough to turn the light on.

Surprisingly, it was nothing like I remembered it. It looked like a completely normal basement, just aged and dusty from years of abandonment. The basement consisted of one large main room--filled with dozens of storage tubs that contained my mother's belongings, my dad's old wood working room, and two other side rooms. My dad's old wood shop was the room I was looking for, but the piles of belongings my mom had left behind stopped me in my tracks. They no longer scared me like when I was a child, but rather peaked my interest.

I gingerly walked over and grabbed a random tub off the pile, setting it on the ground to open. I pried the top off to find the box filled with a countless number of shoes. I picked one up, but then threw it back in the box when I saw rat poop inside.

The next box had numerous documents, receipts, and writings, almost all signed by her. I found a simple receipt with her signature, which was both elegant and readable, and stuffed it into my pocket. It was a rather odd thing to pocket, but I realized that I'd been missing out on these hundreds of artifacts from my mother's life and it gave me a rather sentimental feeling.

By the end of my exploration through all of the boxes, I finally reached for the tub that I had set aside to be opened last. It was the pictures, the same ones that sent me screaming up the stairs years earlier.

Inside the box was hundreds of photos, each one a portal into a different time of my mother's life. Many were from her childhood, some from her teen years, a few with my dad, but photos of her with me were hard to find. Unlike before, I did recognize her, just not in the way you would think. I had no memories of my mom or what she looked like, but something about her face seemed familiar. Then I realized it was like looking in a mirror. I saw myself in my mom. The way her nose slightly curled up at the end just like mine made me yearn for the memories I never got to have with her.

There was no way I could look through every single picture. It was already almost noon and I hadn't even made it into my dad's wood working room--the entire reason I had come down in the first place.

After cleaning up the huge mess on the floor, I made a mental note to come back down soon to look through the stuff more observantly. I was no longer scared of my basement, but instead a little angry at myself for everything I had been missing out on.

I finally made my way into my dad's wood working room to search for the proper materials I needed for Summer's gift. The entire room was covered in a layer of dust, causing allergies to inflame my sinuses. Sniffling, I began digging through piles and piles of unused, perfectly cut pieces of wood.

"Uriah?" my dad yelled from the top of the stairs.

Shoot.

I had forgotten to close the door, exposing my sneaky behavior.

I needed to come up with a plan quickly so I tried buying myself some more time.

"Uh, yeah?"

"Why are you down there?" I couldn't tell if he was angry or suspicious.

"Ummm," I thought of the best excuse possible. "I need wood for a project at school."

There was a few seconds of silence, and I found myself squeezing my fists tightly together hoping he would believe it.

"Okay. Don't be too long. Stay out of mom's stuff," he said and then slammed the door.

I released the tension in my hands as I heard his footsteps above me walking away from the door.

The way he said "mom's stuff" had given me goosebumps. Maybe his coping mechanism with her death was denial. Was that why he couldn't bear to get rid of everything? Did he ever go through her belongings, like I just did, and pretend that she was just on a long business trip?

When was the last time he was down here? I asked myself, never having recalled a time he wasn't in the kitchen, his bedroom, or office.

I shook the thoughts from my brain as they were triggering a headache, and began putting together a rough draft of what I planned on creating. My blueprint looked good, but I still needed a few nails, screws, and paint. That would have to wait for another time, though. My dad was already suspicious. Over the next few days I would need to sneak back down to the basement and pray that he didn't catch me.

Chapter 27

In the days leading up to Valentine's Day, I was able to sneak downstairs a few times without my dad noticing. He spent almost all of his time at home, so I had to attempt it when he was either sleeping or working in his office.

Finally, the day before Valentine's, I finished up Summer's gift with one last stroke of purple paint. I was in a closet inside my dad's wood working room, trying to minimize my chances of getting caught. I didn't know what scared me the most, my dad getting upset at me for sneaking into the basement or him finding Summer's gift. Honestly, I probably would have been embarrassed if anyone but Summer saw her gift.

I set the brush down and admired my masterpiece. It looked absolutely perfect, but it wasn't quite finished yet. It was done as a whole, but a few accessories that were vital to the whole presentation of the gift were still missing. I searched around the basement for what I needed, but as I had feared, I came up empty. I knew that I would have to buy them, but how was I going to get to a store? My dad wouldn't buy these without asking why, and what would I tell him then? For a split second Shane came to my mind, but a piercing memory of our argument extinguished that idea. The only other person I could think of that could drive was Summer.

I settled on walking to a dollar store that wasn't too far away from my house, which caused my leg to throb in pain by the time I arrived. It was not a smart thing to do, but I couldn't think of another option.

I pulled open the door and limped my way into the store. I searched the isles until I found exactly what I needed. I had hoped to buy ten of these, but all the store had in stock was eight so I had to settle. Cradling the objects in my arms, I walked up to the lady at the register, who looked extremely depressed. She stared at my leg for a few seconds, then began scanning my purchases.

"Would you like it in a bag?" she asked in a monotone voice. I almost felt sad just being in her presence.

"Yes, please," I responded politely. It was the least I could do.

It was just past 10 o'clock when I cautiously walked through my front door. I scoped out my house to make sure my dad was upstairs and asleep, then took off for the basement again.

One hour before the official start of Valentine's Day, I declared the gift done and ready for Summer to see. It wasn't too heavy so I would be able to transport it up the stairs the next night after my dad left for the bar to meet up with his old high school friend. Every Valentine's Day my dad and his bachelor friend meet up at their favorite bar to get super wasted and I obviously know why.

This was my first opportunity to have Summer over at my house since we started dating. I had planned the perfect night. We would have the whole house to ourselves, I was giving her the perfect present, and my dad probably wouldn't get home until around one in the morning. We had only ever seen each other at school, the movies, or a restaurant, so I was extremely nervous to see if the special night I had planned ended up being perfect. It would, or at least I hoped it would.

Summer and I had been texting back and forth all night. She had already told me she was going to bed, but I decided to call her anyway. Maybe she would pick up. It rung four times before a gentle voice answered the phone.

"Uriah?" she sounded worried.

"Hi, Summer," I spoke quietly.

"Hi, babe," her voice more clear. "What's up?"

We had been dating for a couple weeks, but when she referred to me as "babe," I still couldn't fully grasp the idea that Summer Harris was *my* girlfriend.

"I just finished your Valentine's Day gift," I told her.

Everything seemed so much more romantic late at night.

"You were up this late working on it?" I could almost see her smiling through the phone. "I can hardly wait."

"It's going to be a perfect night," I whispered.

"I wouldn't want to spend it with anyone else," she matched my hushed tone.

After a few moments, she spoke again, "I will see you tomorrow. Goodnight, Uriah."

I waited a few seconds before replying. The urge to tell Summer I loved her was poking through every inch of my skin. We had only been dating a couple short weeks, but I think I really meant it. I was positive I actually loved Summer for who she was, not just the thought of her. Ultimately, I decided to hold back my first "I love you" as it was almost midnight and I sat on my basement floor talking with her on the phone.

"Goodnight, Summer."

The next morning I woke up extremely relieved that I hadn't let late night emotions get the best of me and embarrass myself by telling Summer I loved her. I usually screwed things up without meaning to, but I had dodged a bullet on this one. It would come, at the right time of course, and I knew I had to be patient.

It didn't take very long before I saw the first girl at school carrying around Valentine's Day balloons and a teddy bear. Undoubtedly, they were probably from her friend, which made it even more awkward. Summer and I took a seat at our normal passing time table, making fun of every girl boasting about their Valentine's Day gifts.

"You could've had all of that!" I mocked a girl carrying a teddy bear larger than herself and a box of heart-shaped chocolates.

"Barf. I can definitely be a really sappy person, but not with this type of stuff," she said as she watched the girl try to walk blindly.

"Perfect. Hopefully you'll love your gift."

"Is it unique?"

"For you? Of course. It has to be."

The bell rang and we headed to our second-hour class, where I would be bored out of my mind. The rest of the day went by a bit faster, with two tests and a presentation, but at 3 p.m. the final bell rang and I was free for the weekend. A buzz in the air emphasized the excitement surrounding Valentine's Day, and it was actually contagious. For a guy who had never been thrilled about this particular holiday, I would have been pacing around my house with excitement if I had I been able to.

My father didn't say goodbye before he left, but that did not bother me too much. He was always worse than usual on days that made him miss mom more so I always stayed clear of his path.

He left at around six, giving me just enough time to prepare for Summer's arrival at 7 p.m. Summer had asked me if six was okay, but I convinced her to push it back an hour to make sure my dad was gone. He probably wouldn't care even if he found out, that's just how distant we were. I didn't want to tell him I had a girlfriend.

After taking a shower, picking out a nice outfit, and shaving my peach fuzz, I had to bring Summer's gift up to the living room, where I had decided I would give it to her. After struggling to get it up each stair, I positioned it perfectly and threw a sheet over it to enhance the mystery.

While waiting for Summer, I started preparing dinner-- something I had never done before. On the menu was my famous "Chips 'n Cheese," tater tots, and chicken poppers. It was nothing special, but it didn't need to be. Summer filled the void. Everything was set and ready to go when the doorbell rang. I hadn't got a text from Summer yet, making me a little anxious to see who was actually at the door.

I wiped my hands free of grease and was walking over to the door when a horrible thought struck me. *What if it was Shane coming over to apologize?* I would have to accept his apology and then ask him to leave when Summer got to my house, stabbing him with the very knife that he had already used to kill our friendship.

I opened the door and was instantly taken back. Summer looked absolutely astonishing.

"'You look…" I tried catching my break without making it noticeable. "Lovely."

For once, she wasn't wearing a hat and her brown hair flowed like a majestic waterfall all the way to her chest. She had applied no makeup to her face, which I honestly preferred. Summer was perfect just the way she woke up in the morning. To top it all off, she wore a velvet, red dress that ended just above her knees, revealing two soft, smooth legs.

"Thank you!" her nose crinkled when she smiled.

"Welcome to my home!" I grabbed her hand as she took her snowy shoes off. "Would you like a tour?"

"Why certainly!" Summer said in a fake British accent.

I proceeded to show her every room of the house: bedrooms, bathrooms, closets, and even my dad's office, but I purposely skipped the basement. I wasn't quite ready to share my mom with anyone else yet, not even Summer. When we ended back up in the living room, she spotted her gift right away but didn't ask, even though I saw her look over at it a few times.

Summer sat on the couch and I went into the kitchen to prepare the room for dinner. I evenly spaced out the three appetizer foods I had made on two of our nicest plates and set them at our dining room table. I then lit two candles that I had found in a kitchen cabinet and placed them in the center of the table, turning off every other source of light in the room.

It wasn't until after finishing our simple Valentine's Day meal that I realized how much better Summer looked in a candle-lit room, if that was even possible. She was so enchanting. I didn't care about the loss I had experienced in my life between my mother and Shane, or the fact that my dad was the way he was, or anything difficult that was yet to come in my life; my only focus was Summer. I had lived my whole life worried about things that I couldn't control and without her even knowing, Summer changed that.

"You are my miracle, Summer Harris," I spoke in an appropriate softness that correlated with the dim room.

"Uriah."

"No, like really, I'm serious. I'm not saying that to be cute or anything, I genuinely mean that meeting you, and us now dating, is my life miracle--the one I thought I would never receive."

I could tell she was blushing now as she replied, "What do you mean?"

"I've never told you this, but before we met, I was crazy about you. I spent day and night thinking about the gorgeous senior who didn't even know who I was. I dreamed of a day that I would be able to even TALK to you, and now look at where I am," I gestured to the date we were currently on. "I was just so lost, you know? Shane was pushing me away, my dad was forcing me to run this stupid track race, and the girl of my dreams was dating the biggest douchebag at our school. I had given up on all hope for happiness, but then everything with my leg happened and I saw you in Ann Arbor that day. It changed everything. You are my miracle, Summer."

"I, um," she was flustered.

I couldn't stop now, I was on a roll.

"No, but you are. You see, only a select amount of people get their own miracle. For some, it's becoming a superstar athlete. For others, it's barely surviving a bad accident. And for some people, it's beating a disease or cancer. But, you always just hear about these miracles; you never really expect to have your own. Deep down you hope that maybe someday you too will receive your own miracle. I had given up all hope on mine but then, miles away from our hometown, our paths crossed and nothing can convince me that seeing you in the parking lot that day was not my miracle."

She looked in love, heartbroken, and flattered all at the same time. And yet, she couldn't find the right words to say.

"I'm sorry if that overwhelmed you," I began to regret my whole speech about miracles, thinking it had been too much. "That probably sounded crazy."

"No," she said looking down at the table. "That was just, um, the most important thing I could have heard tonight."

"It's true. It came from the heart. I'm not making any of this up."

I felt more romantic than I ever had in my entire life.

"I felt so worthless with this whole going to college thing and Davy acting how he did. I felt like I didn't matter to anyone, but hearing that erases every doubt I've ever had."

I grabbed her hand from across the table and she finally looked up. "Nothing is ever going to stop you from being my miracle, I promise."

"Okay, close your eyes!" I knelt down beside her long-awaited Valentine's Day gift. She stood with both hands covering everything on her face but her perfectly shaped smile. I took a good grip of the sheet covering her gift and prepared to pull.

"Ready?" I asked.

"Of course!" she said, her knees swaying back and forth.

"On the count of three!" I said, building up as much suspense as possible.

"One... two...three!" I yanked the sheet and she pulled her hands away from her face.

At first she looked confused on what exactly it was, but then she took a couple steps forward, examined it closer, and gasped.

"Uriah Peterson! You did not!" she was turning red, similar to the shade of her dress.

Standing on the floor before Summer was her very own miniature love bridge. She had mentioned on our first date how badly she had wanted to visit one with Davy, and I knew I couldn't drive her to a real one as a surprise, so I did the best I could to bring it to her. It was long enough for only a few steps and wide enough to fit one person, but it was at least something. Attached to the bridge were eight locks, each with a notecard containing a key moment in our relationship thus far in chronological order. The first was a short paragraph about how we met. The second contained information about our first date. The third marked our first Valentine's Day, and the rest were blank, waiting to be filled.

Summer was giggling in awe, "How did you do this?"

"You like it?" I asked as she came over and gave me a hug.

"Of course. It's magnificent."

"I wanted to take you to a real one..."

"No, I like this one better. It's our very own personal love bridge!" she said, gently rubbing her hand over the creation.

"I think it should be able to fit in your car if you want to take it home," I smiled, watching her admire the gift.

"This is the sweetest thing ever, Uriah. How long did it take?"

"Probably only a few days. I remembered you said Davy wouldn't take you to see it and even though I literally couldn't, I did my best."

"I can't express enough in words how great this is," she said taking pictures of the bridge from every angle.

"I'm glad you like it, babe," joy erupted throughout my entire body. I had been a bit nervous she would think it was cheesy or stupid.

"Here stand next to it!" she instructed me as I shuffled over to my creation and smiled.

"Got it, perfect. This is so cool."

Summer walked over to me and for a split second, I thought her lips were coming for mine, but instead they went right beside my head and before I knew it she was engulfed in my shoulders.

Chapter 28

I've only seen the movie *Forrest Gump* once, and I couldn't tell you what it's about to save my life. It was the movie playing when Summer and I had our first kiss, on my couch, on Valentine's Day 2018, at approximately 9 p.m. I had made popcorn in my kitchen and walked into my living room, where she was getting the movie set up. About two or three minutes into the movie, it was obvious that neither of us really felt like watching it, but we kept it playing as a conversation began.

"When did you realize you first had a crush me?" she asked, facing me criss cross applesauce.

"Um," I had to truly think for a moment. "There was no exact moment. It just gradually happened over time, you know? I just started thinking about you more and more every day."

"That's sweet! And, kind of creepy!" she laughed.

"It is not!"

"I'm just kidding. No, it's not," she said, making me feel better. "Well, maybe just a teeny bit!"

"Oh my gosh, Summer!" I protested and she grabbed her stomach from laughing so hard.

"Fine, fine, it may be a little creepy. Let's hear about you then?" I raised my eyebrows.

"What do you mean?" she wiped her eyes.

"When did you first realized you liked me? Was it gradual also?"

"Oh, gosh no. I had no idea who you were until that one day in the hallway."

"Really? What was your first thought?"

"Well, to be honest, I saw you before Davy did. Your bruised and cut face caught my attention, but then when he started ripping into you, I thought that you were actually pretty cute," she said, shrugging her shoulders.

"So your boyfriend was ripping into a sophomore and his best friend and all you could think about was how cute I was?"

"I'm sorry, Uriah! It's stupid I know."

I could tell that she wished she hadn't said anything.

"You're sorry? That's freaking great!" I was chuckling.

"You aren't mad?" she asked with wide eyes.

"Heck no, not if in that moment you sparked an interest in me!"

"I guess it's not that bad when you think of it that way!"

"So, what happened next?" I asked, eager to hear more.

"I was really conflicted the next few days. I had thought it was nothing more than just thinking you were attractive, but I actually couldn't stop thinking about you and I didn't even exactly know why. You were on my mind constantly, and I felt a little guilty because I had a boyfriend. But then Davy and I broke up and I could freely daydream about you," Summer stared me right in the eyes with every single word she spoke.

"That's crazy," I said. "I mean, something about me just stuck with you?"

"Yes, it was weird. But then, of course, I saw you in Ann Arbor and my stomach literally dropped and I was like 'be cool, be cool.' At that moment I knew for sure I had a thing for you."

"Mind blowing, isn't it? How things work out sometimes."

"Almost like… a miracle," she repeated my words from earlier.

We sat staring at each other for a few seconds, mimicking one another's facial expressions, until I finally said, "You didn't seem nervous at all."

"I was flipping out on the inside."

"Why? It's just me!"

"Exactly, it was you!"

"Can I admit something?" I felt like I could tell her anything. "When I saw you, I asked my dad to go another way."

"Uriah Peterson!" her jaw dropped. "You obsessed over me for weeks and then your opportunity was right there and you were going to let it slip!"

"I know, I know. I just… looked terrible."

"I thought it was pretty adorable, how your hair was all messed up and your leg was propped out," she scooted closer to me, running her hand through my hair.

The touch sent a shiver down my whole body, causing me to tense up in multiple spots. My heart was beating in my throat. *Was it finally going to happen?* Right now seemed like the perfect spot, the perfect time for a first kiss.

I looked her in the eyes, which were giving me the "go for it" green light. I stared back at her, occasionally looking down at her lips, which were coming closer and closer to mine. Without realizing it, I had begun to lean in toward her body. Finally, we hit the point of no return and our lips touched with a gentle, affectionate kiss.

Chapter 29

I was six years old before I ever tried bacon. One day at lunch, this girl asked me if I wanted to try a piece so I took a small bite. It was like heaven. The next few days I went on a bacon binge, eating as much as possible until I finally got sick from eating too much of it and threw up a half dozen times. I haven't consumed one single strip of bacon since.

My kiss with Summer was similar to my bacon craze in some ways. I had never kissed a girl before, but now that I had, it was the most amazing thing in the world and I wanted more. Unlike bacon though, I never got sick of it and each time my lips connected with Summer's, it sent a new jolt throughout my body. I don't know how long we made out. All I know is that when we finally sat up on the couch, the movie was at least halfway over. And, man, was I tired.

We wiped our faces and I just stared at her, smiling. I didn't know how much practice she had, but it was amazing. In fact, I even felt embarrassment at how bad of a kisser I was. Surely she couldn't have enjoyed that as much as me.

I wanted to ask her if I was a terrible kisser or not, but it would totally ruin the passionate moment we had just experienced. I stared at her lips and she stared at mine, until we found ourselves making out again. Her hands wrapped around my face and my hands pressed against the back of her head. I always imagined kissing this passionately would produce a very lustful desire, but it didn't at all. The only emotion I had in that moment was affection for Summer and I felt like nothing could change the way I was feeling.

But then, without any warning, my front door burst open and my dad came stumbling into the room singing very obnoxiously. Instantly, Summer and I quickly separated our faces and I got up from the couch. I began to walk over toward my dad, who was staring at us in confusion, and was super drunk.

"W-w-what's going on, Uriaaaah?" he could barely speak.

"Dad, um, why are you here?" I looked over at Summer, who looked scared out of her mind.

"We got kicked out!" he shouted, leaning against the wall and laughing. "Who, who is that?"

"Um," I looked at Summer and tried to come to with a plan to deceive my drunken father, who was now walking toward my girlfriend.

"Dad, stop!" I took off after him.

"Liz! So nice to see you again, darling! Come give me a kiss, baby."

I couldn't tell whether Summer was more scared or creeped out.

"Dad, no!" I pushed him to the couch before he reached Summer, who was standing frozen in her spot.

My dad fell back onto the couch with a very loud yell, but he didn't get back up. Instead, he just started slurring his words until he finally passed out on the couch.

"Summer, I am so sorry!" I grabbed her hand and walked her to the front door. "He usually doesn't get home for at least a couple more hours. I've never been more embarrassed."

"Uriah, it's fine!" she smiled and rubbed my arm, still looking a little rattled.

'No, it isn't!" I could feel the anger rising inside me like a flame. "My drunken father just tried to make a move on my girlfriend!"

"Seriously, it's no big deal. It just frightened me more than anything. I didn't know what was going on."

"Okay, but I'm not sure I totally believe you," I said, my face burning with humiliation.

"Well, I should probably be going anyway."

"Okay."

"I had a great night," she stroked my cheek.

"I did too. I'm just sorry how it had to end."

"Don't worry about it," she said, kissing me on the cheek before turning around and beginning the walk to her car.

I stood by the door and watched Summer leave. I waited until her car was out of sight before I closed the door, leaning back against it in total distress.

Is she even going to like me anymore? I tried accepting that Summer had just been polite and that, more than likely, my father's outburst would break us up.

I hadn't even told her about my parents yet. She didn't know my mom was dead and my dad was an abusive father who didn't care about me. She must have so many questions, yet she did not ask a single one.

Still leaning against my door, I realized that *I* also had so many questions.

Who was Liz? Why did my dad think Summer was whoever that was?

The night had been flawless and somehow my dad had found a way to ruin it. Everything from our dinner discussion, to her love bridge, to our first kiss made this a night that I would never forget. But still, the dominating event I would always remember was my dad walking in drunk and trying to make a move on Summer.

All I wanted to do was go sulk in my bed for the rest of the night, but Summer hadn't had time to take our love bridge so I needed to move it back to my basement. I walked by my dad, who was still passed out and reeking of alcohol, and began to carefully move the gift back to safety. When I got the bridge back to its original spot in the basement, I covered it with a sheet and made my way back up to my room, where I plopped down on my bed both mentally and physically exhausted.

Chapter 30

The next morning, I woke to a rare winter sunshine gleaming through the window into my room. But even, the bright sky could not enlighten the cloudy feeling inside my head from the night before. I laid on my bed for a while, going through all my social media accounts and debating whether or not to text Summer. Ultimately, I decided to leave her alone for a little bit, but then she texted me.

Summer: A new series just came out on Netflix today and it looks really good. Wanna come over tonight and binge watch?

I was shocked. Summer *really* meant it when she told me she didn't care about what happened. Lifting my spirits, I texted her back.

Me: I'm down. I'll bring some snacks.

Summer: Great. Six sound good?

Me: Yes! See you then, babe!

Suddenly life was okay again, but I still couldn't get over what my father did, even if Summer could. It was another reason I could add to the list of why she was my favorite person ever. Granted, I didn't have many others in my life to compete with her, but I could not realistically imagine someone who was a better quality human being than she was. I tried not to imagine how boring and lonely my life would be had we not been dating.

When I walked downstairs into the kitchen, my dad was drinking his usual coffee and reading the newspaper. I stared at him for a few seconds, but after being completely ignored, I began searching through our fridge for the orange juice.

He must not remember last night at all. I found comfort in the thought of not having to talk about what happened.

After making scrambled eggs and toast, I took my plate and headed for the living room where I could eat alone, away from my dad. Just when I put my hand on the door, he said, "Who was the girl?"

"What?" was the only word I could find to say. He had caught me off guard; I was sure he would not remember.

"The girl last night, who was she?" he asked, still reading the newspaper.

"Wow, you actually remembered some of the night? That's a first," I said, prepared for an argument.

"Uriah, I'm not asking again!" he raised his voice. "Who is she?"

Nostrils flared, I stared him right in the face. "Summer. Her name is Summer Harris. She is my girlfriend."

I expected him to get mad over the fact that I had a girl over without his permission, but that didn't seem to irritate him at all.

"Okay, that's all I wanted to know. Next time I ask you a question, you had better answer the first time," he threatened.

"Or what?" I asked defiantly.

"Or you will get smacked across the face so hard you won't want to go to school the next day," he stood up, now intimidating me a little.

We stared at each other for a few seconds. I wanted to scream at him and tell him how much I hated him, but wisely decided not to. He sat back down and picked up his newspaper.

"Is there something wrong with me asking a question?" he mumbled.

"No," I said quietly. "In fact, I have one for you."

"What is that?" he said like he was invincible to any question.

"Who is Liz?"

"Sorry?"

"Liz. You called my girlfriend Liz and tried to kiss her."

He didn't apologize. He didn't even seem sorry, but rather traumatized. A worried look flooded his face like he was freaking out on the inside. I stared at him, wondering why Liz had caused him this much anxiety.

"Uh," he paused. I had never seen him this distraught.

"Well?" I leaned forward with my eyebrows raised.

He suddenly pulled everything together and took a deep breath. "Your girlfriend looked a lot like Liz, especially when I was drunk."

"Dad, who the heck is Liz?" I was almost yelling.

"Lysette."

"Lysette," everything hit me at once. "Wait, that was mom's name."

"Yeah. I called her Liz. You know before she, uh, died," he was looking down at the floor.

"So, you thought that Summer was mom?" I was bewildered.

"Yes."

I walked out of the room wishing I had never entered it. I was sick to my stomach. My freshly-made eggs and toast didn't even sound appetizing anymore. The fact that my dad tried to make a move on Summer while he was drunk was one thing, but knowing he thought she was mom sent a shiver down my spine--one that didn't leave my body for the rest of the day.

Chapter 31

Time went by really quickly after that eventful Valentine's weekend. I spent almost every single day with Summer. Before I knew it, a couple of days turned into a few weeks and it was already mid-March. Most of our time together was at her house, but she occasionally persuaded me to hang out at my house.

At this point, Summer and I had been dating for almost two months and we had yet to exchange the hidden details regarding our families. The only thing we both knew about one another's family was that we both lived alone with our fathers. I did not know how Summer felt, but I was a little curious where her mom was. Was she dead, like mine? Or had she separated from Summer's dad?

Even though I had many questions, I respected the secrecy that Summer wanted to keep about our families. I was not exactly sure when she would be ready, but suddenly one day in the middle of March I made a simple suggestion that would eventually lead to all the answers to my questions.

      After a long, cold winter, spring had finally arrived and going outside was enjoyable again. I was able to be outside without having multiple layers and a coat on, which was the biggest indication that winter was finally over. Eager to experience the great outdoors once again, I sent Summer a text message.

      Me: Wanna go to the beach today? I want to show you my favorite spot ever.

      She replied nearly a half hour later.

      Summer: Uhhhh, it's a little cold outside yet, isn't it?

      Me: No way, it's so nice out! So you in or no?

      Summer: Sorry, Uriah, I really don't want to.

      It was extremely odd that Summer was acting like this, usually she was always very cheerful and outgoing. I stared at the text for a few minutes trying to decipher why she wouldn't want to go to the beach, but then I accepted defeat. I tossed my phone onto my bed and went to play Xbox.

After a solid 45-14 win on Madden over one of my online friends, I walked back upstairs to grab my phone, finding an unread text from Summer.

Summer: Hey, I got something we can do instead though. Want me to pick you up in like, let's say an hour?

Me: It's nice enough outside. I can walk.

I was still upset that she had rejected my idea, but I never passed on a chance to be with Summer. Plus, I was really eager to see if she was acting just as weird in person. My Xbox filled the time until I decided to leave for Summer's house, and after another solid win I told my buddy I couldn't do a rematch. When I walked outside I felt almost naked not wearing a jacket, but the feeling of natural warmth felt better than ever before. Embracing the beginning of spring, I started walking down my road to Summer's house, which wasn't too far away.

By the middle of March I no longer required my knee brace. My only restriction was absolutely no jogging or running on my leg, which I wouldn't be able to do for months still. While I still went to physical therapy occasionally, my visits became less and less frequent with every coming week. It was safe to say that minus the strenuous physical activities, like running or lifting weights, my leg was completely back to normal.

From a distance I saw Summer's vehicle, and not long after, I found myself walking by the car and into her driveway. Before I could even text her or knock on the front door, she was opening the door to let me into her house.

When you walk into Summer's house there's a hallway that leads directly to the kitchen. To the right of the entryway, there is a large closet where the washer and dryer sit, and to the left is the living room. There is a large, black television mounted just above the fireplace and a brown, leather couch with a matching love seat filling the space. Next to the love seat is a window frame bordering a large window that looks out into their yard and rest of the neighborhood.

Summer's living room was way nicer than mine, but each time I went to her house it gave me an eerie feeling. There were no pictures, paintings, or inspirational quotes hanging up anywhere. Instead, it was just plain beige walls. Her house showed no evidence of a mother or that one had that ever lived there. My house still had artwork and pieces hanging on the walls that must have been my mother's decorations; I know for a fact that my dad would never take the time to hang anything like that up in our house. Every single time I entered Summer's house this thought bounced around in my brain, but I never asked her about it. I wanted to wait until she was ready, and today, she was ready.

"Hi!" she hugged me tightly, as if I had been out of town for a week.

With her head buried into my chest, I wrapped my arms around her shoulders until she pulled away. Right away I could tell that she wasn't angry or upset, but rather just a little gloomy. I would say depressed, but I think you should only use that word if someone is clinically diagnosed as being depressed, not just sad. Sometimes life just sucks, and that's okay because it's not always going to be perfect.

I had never seen Summer genuinely sad before so this was new territory to me.

"How are you?" I idiotically asked her.

"I'm fine," she faked a smile.

Something was definitely wrong, but what was it? Had Davy said or did something to her? Did *I* say or do something?

"What do you have planned?" I asked, feeling a little guilty now for being mad at her earlier.

"It's a surprise," she said in a tone that I could tell wasn't really a big surprise; she just didn't want me to tell me yet.

"Okay, I love surprises!" I lied, trying to do anything to cheer her up.

We walked outside to her driveway and I opened her car door to get in the passenger's seat, but then she stopped me.

"No, don't get in the car," she stopped me. "I want to walk there."

"Oh, okay," I was fine with walking.

Summer led the way down the road and remained silent most of the way. She was so quiet that I almost felt stupid for being in a good mood. I tried starting conversation a few different times, but I never received more than single-worded responses. Accepting defeat, my mind began to wander until it finally asked itself, *"What if she is about to break up with you?"*

But, why would she? Was it because she would be leaving for college that fall and wanted to limit the damage to my heartbreak, or had she simply lost interest?

I didn't know which I would have preferred, but the one thing that I knew for sure was I hoped more than anything in the world she was not going to break up with me. I needed Summer way more than she knew and the thought of losing my only companion felt like a sucker punch to the stomach. Who would I have if she broke up with me? I had made the mistake of not befriending anyone after Shane and I became best friends so the termination of our friendship left me with no one except Summer, who was probably about to end things with me too.

Any normal kid with no friends could probably still make it in life because they would have something that I did not: a family. Unfortunately for me, I did not have this luxury. My father didn't care about me or my life at all except when it came to track. It was even worse at this point in my life when I couldn't run. He just treated me like a soulless human who was living in his house. He never asked how my day was going or if I wanted to go see a movie.

All of these thoughts had forced my heart to beat rapidly with anxiety. I had been looking down at our feet, walking side by side, when her white Converse sneakers came to a stop. I too came to a halt and looked up, not really sure what to expect. My eyes took a couple of seconds to adjust to the sun glaring down on what was an empty playground. I looked over toward Summer, confused. Why had she brought me to a depressing, run-down playground? She was looking right back at me, forcing a smile while in obvious discomfort.

The playground looked like it hadn't been used in years. The metal was starting to rust and many parts of the park were missing or broken. I looked around trying to figure out exactly where we were. I had never been to this playground before but I quickly realized the location. My dad usually drove on the nearby road anytime we would leave town for a track race, but it was usually always dark so I never noticed the abandoned park.

"Want to swing?" she finally spoke.

"Sure!" I said, glad she was actually talking now, even though I wasn't sure I trusted the rusty swings.

For being ancient and plagued with orange rust, the swings were actually pretty enjoyable. Besides the constant screech every time I came forward, they worked like a normal swing should. I had not been on swings in years, so the urge to swing really high came upon me, but I was able to fight the temptation. Summer was slowly rocking back and forth, therefore, it wouldn't be very appropriate of me to swing like a child would. And, that wouldn't be good for my leg.

Mimicking her lethargic pace, I was struck with a question I had never asked Summer.

"What's your middle name?" I broke the silence.

"I don't have one," she looked over at me.

"What!?" I was getting somewhere.

"My parents never gave me a middle name, said they didn't think I needed one," she explained.

"But you've got to have a middle name! It's essential!" I said in disbelief.

"Says who?" she giggled. I had finally broken through.

"Says me!" I raised my eyebrows, then she actually laughed. "I'm giving you a middle name."

"My middle name rests in your hands!"

I thought for a couple of minutes about what would fit well with her name, then it finally hit me.

"Summer Rose!"

"How did I know you were going to pick that!" she leaned her head back in laughter. Summer was slowly breaking out of her shell of sadness.

"What do you mean? That's beautiful!" I proclaimed.

"It is, but just very cliché."

"Well, sorry for trying!" I jokingly frowned as she laughed.

"I like it! I do I promise!"

"No, you just won't have a middle name, I guess!" I played the victim.

"Oh, stop it!" she reached over and grabbed my hand. There was no way she could be breaking up with me.

"What's your middle name?" she said after our hands separated a few seconds later.

"Jay."

"Awh, that's so cute, Uri!"

"It's not bad," I shrugged.

"Uriah Jay Peterson! He just sounds like a handsome guy!"

"Thank you, Summer No-Middle-Name Harris!"

"You've got to admit, *it is* unique," she kicked the wood chips at her feet.

"I'll give you that," I was staring at the ground and I could see her looking at me from the corner of my eye.

"What are you thinking about?" she asked, keeping her eyes locked on me.

Without thinking of a better response, I just said, "Honestly, I am wondering why I'm sitting with my girlfriend on the swings of an abandoned playground."

It was like a switch flipped inside her brain. I had finally gotten Summer back to her normal self, but then she suddenly reverted back to her previous mood. Confused at what I could have said to upset her again, I was ready to hear whatever Summer was about to tell me.

She breathed out a heavy sigh and said, "Uriah, I think I'm ready to tell you about my mom."

Of course… her mom! I felt ashamed that the possibility hadn't even crossed my mind.

"Are you sure?"

"I think so," she was, obviously already in anguish.

"Ten years ago, when I was seven, my parents and I went to North Carolina for Spring Break. I was so excited. What little girl wouldn't be?" I kept my eyes glued to her. "Anyway, one morning we woke up and my dad told me to get my swimsuit on because we were going out on the ocean."

I thought I could see where this story was going, but nevertheless I listened with full attention.

"I still remember how hot it was that day. I can almost feel it right now. I was so excited, Uriah, so eager to stop and jump out on the ocean and be free!" she was starting to get emotional.

Then, it hit her all at once.

"I was so stupid," she cried.

She covered her blotchy, red face trying to fight back against the heart-wrenched sobs.

"Summer, it's okay. You don't have to tell me."

"Yes, I do," she sniffled and somewhat pulled herself back together.

"My dad was driving the boat and he was telling me, 'Summer, stay right by my side, You can wait.' But, I was only seven!" She wiped her face. "And I got mad at how long he was taking and started running to the front of the boat to my mom. But then, the boat hit a big wave and I went flying to the edge."

"Did you fall out?" I asked, hoping it would help to make telling the story easier on her.

"Almost. I remember screaming for help just as a hand grabbed mine and pulled me back in to the boat."

"Your mom?"

"Gosh, no. I wish it was my mom. It was my dad. He left the steering to save me and he didn't get back in time."

"What do you mean?" I asked, confused.

"Supposedly, there was another boat full of a bunch of drunk people that had gotten way too close and my dad hadn't been able to slow down."

She stopped again and tried regaining her composure. I can't explain how tough it was to see her like this.

"We hit right into the side of their boat and all three of us were thrown out into the ocean. I should have died. I know I should have, but I didn't. I surfaced from the water with no more than a headache. I screamed and screamed for my dad and he finally called back out to me."

"Next thing I knew, we were safe on a completely new boat, but my mom was missing," Summer paused for a few moments. "They think she hit her head because a couple of days later they found her dead on the ocean floor."

I had been expecting that type of result ever since she started the story, but there was no way to prepare for the way she told it.

"Summer..." I was at a loss for words, let alone comforting ones.

"I know," she was clearly struggling to hold it all in. "But, it's all my fault."

"No, it's not! It wasn't your fault that they caused the accident!"

I got up from my swing and knelt beside her, wrapping her in my arms.

After a few minutes of silence, still enclosed in my arms, she said, "That's why I brought you here to tell you."

I had become so lost into the story that I forgot we were even at the playground on the swings.

"What?" I didn't see how this had anything to do with her mom.

"Before my mom passed, she would bring me here," Summer stroked the chains of the swing. "Every time we came here, she would push me on this very swing. I loved it so much. I always had a blast. But when my father and I returned back to Michigan, the playground visits suddenly stopped and it sucked."

"Yeah, I understand. I can't imagine how much pain you experienced," I felt like whatever I said wasn't genuine enough.

"When I come here I feel like she's here with me, and it's comforting."

"That makes a lot of sense. I wish I had something like that," I too felt the rustic chains.

"What do you mean?" Summer asked me.

"My mom died too," I said, but without the emotion Summer had.

"I'm so sorry, Uriah." she didn't seem surprised as she rubbed her thumb on my hand. Normally when people tell you they are sorry about something they have no control over, it's just because they don't know what else to say. Summer, though, was different and said it with compassion. Perhaps it was because she actually knew what it felt like to not have a mom.

I went on to tell her the entire story, the one I had been told my entire life--about how my mother was murdered by an intruder when I was only a year old and how I had never formally met her so I have no memories, like a swing set, to share of her.

That part of the story was particularly easy, because I can't recall my mom's death like Summer can, but then I told her about my dad. Summer was the first person that I had ever told about some of the things my dad had done to me. Every new abuse or neglect story I would share made me feel more and more vulnerable, but it felt good to be unleashing everything I had been hiding for years now.

"Uriah, you need to tell someone," Summer looked at me like I had contracted a fatal disease.

"I just did."

"No, I'm talking about the cops or some kind of authority. You shouldn't be living with him if he treats you like that," Summer said, matter-of-factly.

"I guess not, but who would I live with?"

"I don't know," she sat back to think for a minute. "Anywhere but with him, though."

"Maybe," I now wanted this conversation to end as quickly as possible.

After finally sharing our family secrets with each other, I felt a stronger connection with Summer than I ever had before. Still, talking about my "relationship" with my dad felt uncomfortable. She must have sensed that too because she didn't keep insisting I do something about my father. Instead, we sat there in silence once more.

I had always hated silence. I thought it was awkward and weird, but this type of quietness between Summer and I was almost peaceful. The moment we were sharing together was a very special one, yet something was nagging at my brain that I could not hold inside any longer.

"Is that why you didn't want to go to the beach?"

"Yeah," she answered immediately. "I haven't been to one since. You probably think I'm a drama queen, but it's hard."

"No, I totally get it."

"But, it's weird," Summer's voice was perfect. "That is why I chose NC State because she was buried there and I want to be with her. I want to be close to her all of the time. A swing set can only do so much."

"Wait, really?" I hadn't put two and two together.

"Yeah. I know it seems paradoxical because I won't even go to a beach, something she loved, but it's what I want."

"I can't blame you. I don't even know where my mom's grave is."

"Your father never took you to visit it?"

"Nope."

Instead of sympathizing me with more words, she reached over and grabbed my hand. We started swinging, hand in hand, without saying a single word. I don't know how long we stayed like this, but I've never felt more serenity than in that moment.

For the first time that I could recall, I was completely content. Life was perfect.

Chapter 32

But then Summer stopped talking to me.

After no response from my multiple text messages

asking her if she wanted to

have a board game night, I decided to call her. The call

lasted more than a few rings, which made me think her

phone could not have been broken or dead, but yet she still

didn't answer.

Why would she not text or call back? It's one in the

afternoon! I tried examining the situation, but came up with

no logical reason as to why she was ignoring me.

It was very unlike Summer to not respond. Some

people have that type of personality, where they sometimes

take hours to respond, if they remember to respond at all, but

not her. After sending her a text, the longest it usually took

for her to send one back was no longer than ten minutes.

Now, it was coming up on two hours. In desperation, I

scanned all her social media for any type of activity on her

accounts.

My heart sank when I saw that she had "liked" a Tweet that had been posted only forty-nine minutes ago. The urge to send Summer a fourth text asking her to explain how she could like a Tweet but not respond to me surfaced to my chaotic thoughts, but in realization of how crazy I would sound, I chose not to. I just had to wait until she was ready to talk. Leaving my phone on the nightstand beside my bed was tough. I wanted to keep on searching for more activity, but the sane part of me knew I would get nowhere.

After a couple of anxious Madden games, I checked my notifications to find nothing but a lousy Instagram alert telling me someone I followed had posted for the first time in a while.

Summer didn't call or even text me back the entire day, which would create an interesting situation the next day when she would have to face me in our algebra first hour. The reason why Summer was ignoring me remained beyond me, so figuring out what had changed since our talk on the swings was my top priority. When Summer and I sat in silence at the playground, life had felt completely perfect. Obviously the feeling wasn't mutual.

The combination of decent weather and a somewhat healthy leg prompted my father to make me walk to school again. A short and slow walk that morning got me to my high school, which was buzzing with hundreds of kids who had way too much energy for a Monday morning.

Mrs. Wooten opened the door simultaneously with the five-minute warning bell. I entered with a quick "hello" and sat down in my normal seat. Because I was the first student to arrive in the classroom, the wait to see Summer was prolonged another five minutes.

Similar to the first class period I ever had with her, Summer still hadn't arrived when the passing time bell rang for a second time. I should have known that she wasn't going to show up. Of course she wouldn't; it was just my luck.

I waited the entire class in hopes she would walk in, but to my disappointment, she never showed up. I decided now that it was reasonable to text her again.

Me: Summer, please tell me what is going on.

Nothing.

I kept an eye out for Summer in the halls all day long, but by lunchtime it became pretty evident that she wasn't even at school.

Have you ever heard of the saying, "You don't know what you have until it's gone?" I had never experienced the feeling of loss, for my mom died when I was one and I had been raised by my dad only ever knowing neglect. Therefore, I never fully understood what this saying meant. Until now. Until Summer broke off all contact with me. I had become so accustomed to telling her all the little things about my day, or random facts about me, or stories from the past, that when I couldn't tell her anymore, I felt like exploding.

Summer still hadn't responded to my texts or shown up at school after two days, so I decided to take immediate action. She couldn't possibly ignore a visit to her house.

As I slowly walked in the direction of her street, I scrolled through her social media like a stalker to make sure that she was still active, and she was. Summer hadn't posted or tweeted anything, but if you dig deep enough into someone's profile, you can tell whether or not they have been using the app.

The usual doubt that appears when I need to make an important decision arrived right when I got to her driveway. But instead of stopping to think whether or not I should do this, I trudged right up her driveway and straight to her front door. My body was filled with anxiety and excitement at what waited behind that door. On one hand, Summer could refuse to talk to me and I'd never have an explanation, but on the other hand, this visit could persuade her to let me be a part of her life again.

I raised my left fist and knocked three times on the front door. I stayed perfectly silent, except for my racing heartbeat, trying to listen for any commotion inside of the house. The only sound I heard was her dog, the one who had been with her father the night he saved me. A few seconds later, I heard the locks on the door shift and then the door handle turn.

It was Summer's dad.

"Oh, hi, Uriah!" he smiled with the same kindness he had shown me the night he found me on the ice.

"Hi, Mr. Harris," I was hoping it would not have been him. "Is, uh, Summer here?"

"Yeah! Let me go get her real quick!"

He left the door open as I heard him trot up the stairway calling out Summer's name.

It remained quiet for a few moments, but then I could gradually hear the trot get louder again until he was back at the door.

"Hey, she'll be down in a couple minutes! How's your leg?"

He crossed his arms and leaned against the door frame, non-verbally expressing that I would not be invited into the house to wait for her. He was obviously buying time for Summer. This man was way too nice to keep me standing out on his doorstep.

"It's doing great. I can do almost anything, well, except running," I nodded my head and bumped my closed fists together.

"Terrific, and how about your face?" he leaned in to try and get a better look at the white scar alongside of my face.

"Yeah, just a scar now," I felt the altered skin below my eye.

"Do you plan on running after your leg is healed?" he asked.

Ever since my surgery all I had thought about was his daughter, so I had not given any thought to whether or not I wanted to run track anymore. My dad knew he obtained no control over a doctor's instructions and he hadn't bugged me much about it. Deep down, I didn't want to run track ever again, but I knew my father would make me.

"Maybe, I haven't decided---" I started, but then Summer appeared behind her father.

"Ope," he got of Summer's way. "I'll let you two be. Good talking to you, Uriah!"

Summer was still in her pajamas and her hair, while messy, still looked as gorgeous as ever. She stared at me with a look of guilt as she took two steps forward and closed the door behind her. I crossed my arms waiting for a much-needed explanation, but Summer just continued to stare right back at me. She had ignored me for days now and all she could do was stare at me?

"So?" I leaned forward. "What is up?"

"I'm sorry," she said with little emotion.

"Why have you stopped talking to me?" I clearly had to be more assertive.

Summer took her eyes off my face and looked down right at the ground. The look on her face was easy to read: whatever she was about to tell me wasn't going to be good.

"Uriah, you are amazing, and like the best possible boyfriend I could ever ask for, but this just isn't going to work out."

Ouch.

"Why? What changed? You couldn't have told me this right away? You..." I completely unleashed my confused anger.

"Uriah, I'm going to college in five months and I don't want a larger heartbreak than I can control. It's best if we just end things now."

"Summer, I don't care."

"No, you don't understand..."

"No, I do understand. You're scared, and heck, Summer, I'm scared too, but we can't just call this whole thing quits already. I would rather have these next five months with you and endure a greater heartbreak than to have our story finish like this."

Summer stared at me, and she knew I was right, but her look of stubbornness told me I hadn't yet persuaded her.

"Summer, you are my everything, and, no, I'm not just saying that to be sweet or romantic or cute. You are literally everything I have and all that I need, but if you decide to walk out on me, I'm nothing."

"Uriah, that's not true," she muttered.

"You know it is!" I could feel the frustration inside me rising like a volcano. "I lost my best friend, my dad doesn't give a crap about me, my mom's dead, and now you have decided to completely ignore me! You know how much that sucks?"

Tears were now welling up in her eyes and while I felt guilty for making her cry, she chose this, not me.

"Uriah, I don't want to do this, but you aren't the only one hurting right now."

"What do I have to do to convince you that I DO NOT CARE IF YOU ARE GOING TO COLLEGE! I WANT TO BE WITH YOU, SUMMER HARRIS!" I was yelling now.

She twisted the doorknob behind her back and started to walk back inside her house.

"Uriah, I'm sorry. I truly am."

And, just like that, she closed the door on me and on our relationship.

Chapter 33

It was one in the morning, and even though I had to wake up for school early in the morning, I sat in my basement staring at the love bridge I had made for Summer. I felt stupid for even making it. It turned out to be just a big waste of my time and effort. At the time, it had been a great proclamation of love for my girlfriend, but now having it rot away in my basement only served as a symbol of what Summer and I could have been. When I looked at the miniature bridge, I was reminded of the short, but amazing, time we shared together.

My body was telling me that I needed to be upstairs in my bed and sleeping, refueling for the next day, but my mind told me that sitting next to this love bridge was some kind of therapy. I hated being next to the bridge, but for some reason, I couldn't leave its side.

I grabbed the first three locks and read what I had written on each note card, sympathizing with myself for all the hard work I put into this, but then my self-pity was replaced with anger. I stood up and walked over to where my dad kept all of his tools. I searched for the biggest hammer I could find and walked right back over to the bridge in the closet, where I began smashing it in every way I possibly could. Every damaging contact the hammer made with the wood released the frustration, anger, and sadness I had been feeling over the past couple of days. When all of the wood had been broken into bits and pieces, I took the first lock and tried to smash it, but could only manage to create a few dents.

I felt immediate remorse toward what I had just done, but it had given me an escape from everything I was enduring. The smashed bridge was finally enough to release me from my attachment to the basement. After a swift walk past my drunken father and up the stairs to my bedroom, I found myself slowly falling into a sleep that would last until my alarm clock signaled the start of a new day.

The emotions I felt just six short hours earlier did not carry over to the next morning when the repeating beeps of my alarm clock sounded. Instead of feeling anger and frustration, I was overwhelmed with heartbreak and sadness. The fact that Summer and I had dated for only two months in no way affected the severity of my heartache. I had dreamed and dreamed about this girl for weeks and woke up from that dream to find myself actually dating Summer, but now it had turned into a nightmare. Summer was finally able to reveal to me a secret she had hid from me for weeks. By the next day, everything was over.

I hoped that maybe Summer would text me back after I confronted her in person, but after I sent her a text asking "What changed?" I still received no reply.

Even though I knew I wouldn't get a reply, I sent a follow-up text knowing she would still see it.

Me: I guess I will never get to know, but I hope you know it sucks having someone open up that much to you and then the very next day be treated like a stranger.

I thought I had gotten used to Summer rejecting my text messages, but every time she remained silent I only missed her more and more.

Later that night when it became unbearable, I decided to take action. On my bed was the laptop my school had assigned me for the year, so I flipped it open and began researching facts about North Carolina State University (NC State). After close to an hour of research, I had created a Google Doc with, in my opinion, the top five reasons NC State is the best college to attend. My five reasons included sports, academics, campus life, and other programs. I clicked print and I heard my printer downstairs begin to hum. I slammed my laptop shut and headed for the printer. By the time I arrived downstairs, the printed list was waiting on me.

I stood at the end of Summer's driveway with a text message ready to send. My thumb tapped the green box labeled "send" and I alternated looking from her house to my phone, searching for any kind of response. I was re-reading the text I had sent telling her to look outside when I saw movement come from an upstairs window. The shade previously covering her window was now gone, and Summer stared at me from one story above.

I gestured for her to come outside, and at first I thought she was about to pull her shade back down, but then she disappeared from her window and two minutes later she met me at the edge of her driveway. Summer slowly walked right up to me and wiped her face with her sleeve, but not before I saw remnants of her tears.

"Uriah…"

"No, just listen to me!" I demanded her attention. "Give me five minutes."

She looked at the paper in my hands and then sighed, "Okay."

"Let's go for a walk."

She followed me down her street, but remained a step behind the entire time. When I decided the two of us were far enough away from her home, I lifted up the paper.

"Five reasons why NC State is a great college," I expected her to protest, but she let me freely continue.

"Number five: It's home is North Carolina, one of America's most beautiful states."

"Uriah…"

"Number four: NC State has Division 1 athletics and is most well-known for its basketball team, which makes the NCAA Tournament almost every year."

I looked over at Summer, who had tears in her eyes again.

"Number three: this college is 131 years old, originating in 1887. Number two: NC State offers a wide variety of majors and minors."

I then crumpled up the paper and Summer looked at me in confusion. I waited for her to ask about number one, but after a few moments of nothing, I continued.

"Number one: an amazing girl I know, Summer Harris, will attend there in the fall."

For the first time in ages, a small smile blossomed across her face. The smile had given me the happiness that had been absent in my life over the past few days. But all good things must come to an end and the smile met its doom way too quickly.

In fact, Summer's life would meet its end too quickly.

"Uriah," tears began to roll down her face. "I'm not going to NC State."

"What?" I asked, oblivious. "What college are you going to?"

"I'm not going to college. I never was. It's always been a cover up."

"Summer, what's going on?" I was becoming scared at how hard she began to cry.

"College isn't college. College is dying. I'm dying, Uriah."

Chapter 34

I had been in pain many, many times in my life, but the day Summer told me that she had brain cancer was by far the most excruciating pain I had ever experienced. Every single word she spoke served as a fatal blow. The paper containing the reasons why NC State was a great college, now irrelevant, was crumpled up a few inches from my feet and my eyes were gazing off in the distance at a pine tree, praying that this wasn't real, that it was just a bad dream. I can't recall everything Summer told me because my mental state had been stunned, then viciously attacked. But it went something like this.

In early December, right around the time I officially proclaimed my love for Summer, she had visited the hospital for an MRI after her doctor expressed concerned about her poor vision and constant headaches. The MRI results showed a tumor. Still hopeful for a positive prognosis, doctors made Summer an appointment with specialists in Ann Arbor to further examine the tumor.

Everything started making sense to me, all the pieces of the puzzle were fitting together. Summer had told me she had been in a bad place, but it wasn't because Davy had made her feel bad about college; he had made her feel bad about dying. I never once thought about WHY Summer was in Ann Arbor that day, but she had been walking into the hospital to find out whether her tumor was malignant or benign.

When the doctors informed Summer and her dad that she had stage 4 brain cancer that had already spread all throughout her body, they estimated that she had maybe a year to live. Summer tried taking the positive approach and decided to live what was left of her life to the fullest, which explains why she was so friendly to me that day. That is the best mindset to have in theory, but it's just not reality. Summer met me and she didn't think it would be anything more than a friendship, but after I made romantic gestures, such as a love bridge and telling her that she was my miracle, she found herself at a point of no return.

So she decided to tell me about her mother, and once she did, it terrified her. The new level of personal attachment she had just created through telling me her biggest secret (well, second biggest secret), was a bond she deeply regretted, knowing that her own death was imminent. That's why Summer broke off all contact with me, not because she was trying to spare my broken heart, but hers.

"Uriah," she said, tears still rolling down her wet face. I had been able to interpret everything she just told me, yet I could not remember a single word she said.

I broke my stare with the pine tree, and while the pain remained in full effect, the shock began to wear off. I lifted my head toward Summer and as much as I hate to say it, I immediately looked at her in a different way.

"No," my voice quivered. "You can't be dying. You're only seventeen."

"I know," she walked into my arms, crying. "But death knows no age, Uriah."

For the first time in years, I began crying. I forgot how painful sobbing actually felt.

"You can't leave," I struggled to catch my breath. " I won't let you."

She didn't tell me that she was going to fight hard and beat cancer or that maybe she would be that one person who receives a life-saving miracle, because how could she? Can you realistically ever be that optimistic with stage 4 brain cancer that has spread to the rest of your body?

"Does it hurt?" I asked, our bodies both shaking from fear, anger, and sadness.

"Yes. Sometimes," she replied, sniffing in my arms.

I grabbed her head and carefully stroked her hair, not knowing the specific details to the amount of pain she was already experiencing. I don't know how long I stood out on the road with Summer wrapped in my arms, but I knew that no matter the amount of time, I couldn't make this better. They say time heals everything, but no time frame would ever make this okay.

Eventually, Summer and I were able to pull ourselves together enough to where we could walk back to her house. I felt like I was going to puke all over her front door mat as we walked up to the door.

"Summer," I needed to say this regardless of the fact that I could throw up any second. "Don't you ever distance yourself from me like that again. I am going to stay here with you until the very end."

"Okay," Summer found a way to smile in the middle of the darkest period of her fleeting life.

Chapter 35

I wish I could say that I was able to keep it together and be strong for Summer, but I wasn't. In the months leading up to Summer's death, I was cast out into the deepest depression one could ever imagine. Of course, I tried to be happy, and I tried to make the most of my limited time with Summer, but it was inescapable.

Outside of the hours I had to spend at school and sleeping, I spent every other minute of my time at Summer's house. We were still able to do fun stuff, like see movies, eat out at restaurants, and go on walks, until early May, when her health rapidly started declining.

One day, I had gone through my normal after-school routine of going home, dropping off my backpack, and quickly going over to Summer's house, when she had been waiting for me outside in her front driveway.

"Uriah Jay Peterson!" Summer gleamed like she wasn't deteriorating physically and mentally. Summer was the one dying, and yet I was the most depressed. It is one of the biggest regrets I will ever have.

"Summer Harris," I walked up to her and gently kissed her lips. "What's the occasion?"

"We are doing something special today!"

"Half-off appetizers?"

"Even better!"

"How dare you?" I couldn't help but smile at her tiny giggle.

Small and happy moments like these were ones that killed me the most. All I could ever think about was how limited those moments were. I always wondered exactly how many of them we had left. Was it five? Fifty? Five hundred?

"We are going to the beach today!" Summer rubbed her hands together in a nervous gesture.

"Are we really?" Amidst my depression I had forgotten my craving to see the therapeutic water and sunsets.

"Indeed we are. Life's too short to be afraid of anything. I want to see the beach."

Life *is* too short, and even shorter for Summer.

"Let's get to the beach, Summer Harris."

I had not been to the beach since the previous September, and while I was extremely eager to get back to what I loved, I just wished it was under different circumstances. Still, I was proud of Summer for not letting the idea of looming death stop her. Until she could go no longer, she made the most of her life.

Summer's house was about fifteen minutes away from the closest beach. We arrived with an hour to spare before sunset. Sitting in the parking lot, I observed Summer, who clearly was anxious about being there.

"You ready?" I grabbed her hand.

"Yes."

There had only been a couple of other cars in the parking lot when we pulled in, but by the time Summer and I finally got out of her car, we were the only ones at the small beach. My favorite beach.

"I have to take you to this spot. The view is awesome," I said, remembering a location that Shane and I always used to visit.

The path to the water included many stairs and even a few sandy hills, which forced Summer, who was often dizzy and fatigued from her cancer, to take breaks and sit down for a few minutes at a time. When we finally arrived at the spot, the sun was preparing to set.

"Wow," Summer breathed heavily. "This is an amazing."

The spot I brought her to was a small cave atop the beach's largest hill. The sand had eroded away underneath the ground, leaving a sand floor and a dirt roof. Safe in our little cave, we could see for out for miles and miles along Lake Michigan.

"This is an amazing view. I can't believe I have missed out on this kind of stuff my entire life," Summer said. She looked beautiful and at peace.

"Yeah."

The thought of her having to miss out on the beach for the rest of her life haunted me.

Summer sighed, not because she was tired, but rather annoyed.

"Uriah, stop!" she grabbed my thigh.

"Stop what, Summer? You are dying. There is no way I can stop thinking about it!"

"But that doesn't mean you stop living, right? My months, heck, my *weeks* are limited, and I am going to spend them living. I hope you can too."

"I'll try."

I could feel myself starting to choke up, so I refrained from saying anything else.

In that moment, I decided I had to put all of my efforts into finding happiness, even though it was the most difficult thing to come by these days.

"Uri, I'm scared," Summer looked out at the endless waves crashing along the shore.

"So am I."

"No, not like that," Summer stopped me. "I'm scared about you."

"Me?" I subconsciously pointed to my chest.

"What are you going to do when I'm gone? If you are acting like this now, I can't even imagine what it'll be like when I die."

The way she said 'die' made me shudder.

I had been thinking about this a great deal and now seemed like the perfect moment to release everything trapped inside of my head.

"Summer, I can't answer that. When you're gone, I don't know how I'm going to get through my days. My life will be hell. I am nothing without you. When you're gone, what's the point?"

"Uriah."

"No, I'm serious," I had reached the point of no return. "I don't see a reason why I should be even be here. If you are gone, shouldn't I be too?"

Tears flooded my stinging eyes and through my blurred vision, I could see the exact same thing happening to her.

"That's not true," she sniffed. "You have given me happiness in my last months, which otherwise I would not have had. What if someone else needs that in the future and you aren't there for them?"

What she said was true, but it just made me cry harder.

"I'll try, for you," I wiped the wetness off of my face. "I don't how, but I will."

"You need something to help you cope," Summer suggested.

"I have always wanted to try smoking weed."

"Uriah, not like that!" we both laughed amidst our tears.

"What do you suggest?"

"You could write," she answered.

"What? I'm not a very good writer."

"So, you don't have to be! You can write how you are feeling in a journal or write about the times we had together, a way to like vent, you know?"

"Maybe. I can try," I told Summer, even though the idea didn't interest me.

"Wait, no!" Summer and I were so engaged in this new conversation you wouldn't have known that we had been bawling our eyes out just two minutes earlier. "I know what you can do!"

"And, what is that?" I curiously asked.

Her excitement was contagious.

"Write a book!"

"A book?"

"Yes! Write about how we met and about our relationship, and write anything and everything about us that you can think of. Uriah, write *our* story!"

"I'm not that great of a writer, but I will do it."

"I don't care. You promise me?"

"I promise."

Summer had a way of turning sad moments into happy moments in a matter of minutes. No matter the amount of sadness or pain, nothing ever ended on a sorrowful note. Looking back on that day, when Summer and I discussed the future in that small cave at the beach, I remember it only as another happy time that we were lucky to spend together.

Once we had forgotten about every single problem we were facing or were about to face, Summer and I sat and enjoyed the setting sun. The sky was splattered with different shades of red, orange, pink, and white, and I realized how much I missed these sunsets. It was the first time I learned to be content with life and be happy where I was, watching the stars that were millions of miles away sink beneath the wavy water beside my gorgeous girlfriend.

Chapter 36

"How cold do you think that water is?" Summer asked me well after the sun had completely vanished from the sky.

"Very," I shivered at the thought.

"Yeah, probably," she stood herself up. "Let's go swimming."

"What?" I asked, even though I'd heard her perfectly fine.

"I want to swim! I haven't swam in a large body of water in ten years!"

The absence of the sun had already made it colder outside and I really didn't feel like freezing myself half to death, but there was no way I would tell Summer no. So, I followed her down to the water. I hadn't even slipped off my first shoe when Summer was already shoulder-deep in the water. I had planned on testing the temperature on my feet first, but now that she had shown me up, I had no choice but to follow.

"Just come on already, pansy!" Summer mocked me from the water.

I had to do this; what better test of my attitude than jumping into freezing cold water at night?

The water was so cold that I felt icy even inside my lungs. Every sensory neuron screamed across my skin and I was sent into an immediate shiver as soon as my body came back up to the air. I wiped my eyes to see Summer standing right in front of me, fully clothed and shivering just as hard as me.

"Wow, this is cold!" she couldn't stop smiling.

"It's terrible," I smiled back through the chatter of my teeth. "But fun."

"SO MUCH FUN!" she looked like a little kid who had never swam before, splashing around the water. "We have to come back."

"We will! But for now, I think we should get out. We'll come back when it's a little warmer."

It took me a couple of minutes to persuade Summer to leave the water, and once I was finally successful, we made our way back to her car, soaking wet. Due to a few rest breaks for Summer on the walk back, we were somewhat dry by the time we arrived to her car.

"Do you have any towels or something in your car?" I asked before getting into the passenger's seat.

"Nope," she said, hopping right into the car. "Who cares if it gets wet? Not me!"

Uncomfortably, I sat down in the car and continued to shiver while Summer started the car, turned on some heat, and began to drive away. I listened to her talk about how amazing the beach was and how she regretted always being too afraid the entire way home. Summer stopped in my driveway, but wouldn't let me out of her car until I assured her we would take another beach trip soon.

"Uriah, I am serious! We need to go again and it has to be soon!"

"Summer, calm down!" I chuckled. "I promise we will go again."

"Good," she leaned in and pecked me on the lips. "I can't wait."

"Neither can I!"

I did not want to leave Summer, but my body kept reminding me that I had to.

"Bye, Uriah," she kissed me again.

"Bye, Summer."

Later that night while I was lying in bed, I wished I wouldn't have been such a chicken and had stayed in the water longer. I told myself it was okay because Summer and I would definitely be going back for another late-night swim. Unfortunately, we never got the chance.

Chapter 37

I told my father about Summer's brain cancer just a few days after she told me. I didn't really want to tell him, but felt that I had to. My girlfriend was dying and no matter how much I detested him, he needed to know. Honestly, I had expected a lot less sympathy from him than the little he actually showed.

"That's unfortunate, Uriah," he said like he was giving his condolences to a stranger. "I'm very sorry to hear that."

Any normal kid would have wished for a more emotional, supportive response from their father, but I was content with him at least acting like he cared--this is my dad we are talking about. He had never met Summer while sober, but you don't have to be a brainiac to know that anyone who has lost a loved one can sympathize with someone who is about to go through the same thing. It was somewhat nice to know my father had at least one positive quality. I thanked him for his condolences and, like every other day, went over to Summer's house.

I would not have another legit conversation with my father for a long time after that. My days included waking up, going to school, coming home for a quick five minutes, and then spending my whole night with Summer. By the time I got home every night, my father was either passed out drunk or asleep already.

One day, weeks later, I routinely walked into my house and grabbed a snack when my father came walking into the kitchen, gleaming from ear to ear.

"Hey, Uriah, I've got some great news!"

I knew from the rare happiness he was showing that it could only mean one thing.

"What?" I asked, already knowing the answer.

He pulled out his iPhone and made a couple of taps and swipes.

"Coach Brothers is holding some running sessions in a few weeks. I already signed you up and have informed Coach Brothers you cannot run, but you can get started on some easier stuff. Are you excited?"

No, I wasn't excited. My girlfriend was slowly getting worse with every passing day. I hadn't even thought about running for weeks now, and I did not plan to. My mental calendar informed me that a few weeks meant summer vacation, which meant really close to Summer's last days. The last thing I intended to do was fake running exercises for a sport I despised.

"Dad, I would love to get back at it," I lied, "but I need to be with Summer right now."

The joy on his face literally melted and fell off of his face.

"Uriah, it's an hour for a couple days a week. I think you spare some of your time," he snorted. "You are going."

"No," I looked at him more serious than ever. "I am not."

Maybe it was the amount of pain I was in at that time of my life, maybe it wasn't, but for some reason I was suddenly unaffected by the look he gave me--the one that was always followed by a slap to the face. Instead of shying away this time, I actually took a step forward.

"I say what goes around here," he replied, anger rising in his voice. Even though I saw it coming, I had no time to dodge his flying hand. "You are going," he demanded.

I can't even begin to name enough adjectives to describe how much hatred I felt for my father in that moment. Each time he had physically abused me I had been angry, but this time was completely different; I had already been dealing with enough. I stared at him with rage in my eyes, until with one swift motion my hand struck his prickly face and returned the favor.

He turned his reddened face back to mine with a look that was mixed with shock, embarrassment, and pique. He responded not with words, but instead a lunge toward me. This time I was able to react, only allowing him to grab my right arm. His grip was strong and I could feel his nails digging into my forearm as I tried to pry his hand off of me. Before I could get out of his grasp, a right hook was coming straight for my nose, but I quickly dodged his punch. This left his entire lower body open and I took the most of my opportunity, tackling him into the counter. After numerous scratches, shirt rips, and even one solid punch to his right eye, he finally gathered enough strength to throw me off him and over to the other side of the room.

We both had our hands on our knees and were heavily breathing. I could see a bruise forming around his right eye, two red scratches on his neck, and his t-shirt was ripped where the arm connects to the chest. I, on the other hand, had only a ripped collar, along with the fading sting from the original slap.

"Your life is going to be hell, Uriah. You can kiss your precious little dying girlfriend goodbye. You aren't allowed to leave the house except for when you have to run. Hear me?" he smiled and I could actually see blood in his mouth.

"No," was all I said.

"What did you say?"

"I said no. I will never run track again. I HATE IT!" I yelled.

"Are you kidding me? I know you love it, deep inside, but you have let this girl screw up your brain almost as much as hers!"

That did it. I lunged at him and with one hard jab to his jaw, flattened my father to the ground. When he stayed on the ground clenching his jaw, I took the opportunity to kneel down and get right up in his face, where I could smell his sour breath.

"DO YOU HEAR ME? I WILL NEVER RUN TRACK AGAIN. IT IS DEAD TO ME. YOU ARE DEAD TO ME! DON'T CALL YOURSELF MY FATHER BECAUSE YOU HAVE NEVER BEEN ONE TO ME!" I screamed into his face.

"URIAH!" he yelled through the blood in his mouth, but I stood up, stepped over him and ran to my room.

My heart rate thumped at rapid speed as I packed my bag. At any moment I expected my father to come into my room for a verbal or physical rematch, but he didn't. Instead, he was attending to his beaten face in the downstairs' bathroom. But once he heard my footsteps coming down the stairs, he met me at the bottom of the staircase.

"What do you think you are doing?" he tried looking intimidating despite his deranged face.

"I am not staying here," I walked right past him and to the door.

"She means nothing anymore. You have so much potential. Your life will continue, even though hers isn't."

"I'm sorry you feel that way, but she means everything to me," I said calmly even though what he just said was so vile. "You will never change my mind."

"You will see eventually. I just hope she dies soon so it doesn't set you back too far."

Though there was a hundred different ways I desired to inflict pain upon my dad in that moment, I decided to restrain myself from any further arguing or fighting. I took one last look at the man who called himself my father and without looking back, I slammed the door to what I had once called home.

Chapter 38

Summer's father welcomed me into his home without hesitation, which I would have found very hard to do if the roles were reversed. I would have wanted to spend my daughter's last days alone with just her (and the dog), instead of sharing the time with some boy who had only been around a few months.

When I knocked on Summer's front door, her dad answered with his usual smile and invited me in. I asked where Summer was and when he told me that she was sleeping, we sat down at the kitchen table and I told him what had just happened.

"Uriah, are you okay?" he searched my body for any visible signs of injury.

"Yeah, I'm perfectly fine. He looks way worse than I do," I felt proud telling someone that. "But I just have one really important question."

"Of course," he raised his eyebrows.

I thought I had been ready to pop the question, but instead I barely managed to squeak it out. "Can I stay here?"

"I wouldn't let you stay anywhere else, kid," he heartwarmingly smiled at me.

Summer woke up at six that night and she responded with more emotion than her father, despite her dwindling energy.

"We need to call the police," she got out of her humongous bed and yelled downstairs. "DAD!"

"No!" I rushed over to the door and closed it. "It will just make everything worse. Who knows where the authorities will take me. I want to be right here."

Summer 'never minded' her father and after only a little bit more convincing, she agreed that not doing or saying anything would be best right now.

"But what if he calls the police or comes here?" she asked a few minutes later as we set up a game of Monopoly.

"He won't. Hopefully he's smart enough to know he'd only be turning himself in."

"Okay," I saw relief take over her puffed face.

In the two months that I had known Summer before she told me about her brain tumor, I never suspected or noticed any signs of her disease. But in these last few months of her life, I could see her gradually getting worse every day. Her days and nights were never without headaches, trouble swallowing her food, or constant drowsiness. She tried to stay positive, but with every single minute, the tumor took more and more life out of her.

Still, she was focused on finishing out high school like a normal senior. The last couple of weeks were tough, but when the seniors' last day arrived, Summer had finally reached her goal. All the soon-to-be graduates cheered throughout the halls, but instead of joining along with them, Summer and I held hands as we walked toward the back of the school.

"You finally did it, Summer Harris," I kissed her on the forehead. "I'm so freaking proud of you!"

She scrunched up her shoulders and absorbed my kiss, but didn't say anything. When she was standing up or moving around, she didn't say a lot anymore; it was just too hard on her. Her steady decline was hard to watch. I didn't know if she noticed it herself, so I tried to act like everything was normal.

We were taking our sweet time walking in the empty hallway toward the back of the school, when suddenly I heard distant footsteps. I ignored the sound and kept making small talk with Summer, but when I heard the steps turn the corner into our hallway, I looked over my shoulder and saw Davy Trick walking in our direction. From the expression on his face I could tell he hadn't been searching for *me*, but that didn't stop him from saying what he did.

"Ah," he laughed. "There he is. Finally found out did you, buddy?"

"Yeah, I did," was all I could say.

"She made a mistake breaking up with me," he motioned his hips with a sexual movement. "I could have enlightened her last days."

I took a step toward Davy, but Summer wisely stopped me.

"What's wrong with you?" I yelled and silent tears fell from Summer's eyes.

"Sorry 'bout it!" Davy was slowly walking toward me. I didn't understand how someone could be that terrible, that horrific, that they would make fun of a dying girl with sex jokes. I surmised that the only possible reason he was acting like this was out of remorse for screwing things up with Summer, but anyone who could say something like that deserved to rot in hell.

"I'm sorry that you aren't the man I am," I growled.

"Ha, please, you twig," Davy shouted. "You'll never be like me."

"I wouldn't dream of it. I would hate to have wet the bed for as long as you did," I said and Summer chuckled.

He turned to Summer with his face beaming red, "YOU PROMISED YOU WOULDN'T TELL ANYONE! I KEPT YOUR SECRET!"

I turned to Summer and I could see a storm brewing inside of her.

"YOU FREAKING ASKED ME HOW MUCH LONGER YOU COULD TRY HAVING SEX WITH ME BEFORE I DIED!"

I was clearly not the only one surprised at her yelling, as Davy actually took a step backwards. We could hear someone else walking down the hall so out of fear of being caught, he quickly walked up to us and whispered, "This never happened. Have a good rest of your life, whatever little of it is left!"

I had held myself back as long as I could and for the second time in a short span of time, I found myself entangled in a fight. Clearly catching Davy by surprise, I was able to wrestle him to the ground. But once we both got back to our feet, his punches became too much for me and I could no longer put up a fight with him. I could see Summer trying to pry him off of me, but through a blurred vision, I saw Davy shove her out the way as he continued to ram his fists into my body.

Just when the pain became unbearable, I was rescued. Not by Summer, not by some freakish superpower I had unknowingly possessed, but by the person Davy had heard walking down the hallway just seconds before we began fighting.

Suddenly, Davy wasn't on top of me anymore. Instead, all I saw was two bodies wrestling next to me. I clutched my ribs as I crawled to the wall and when my vision fully came back to me, I could see who my rescuer was.

Shane was putting up a good fight, despite being much smaller than Davy. At first, they swapped turns rolling on top of each other, throwing out as many punches as they could before the other would regain superiority. But then Shane jabbed his elbow right into Davy's neck and it was the shot Shane needed to get an edge. Davy had enough strength, however, to throw Shane off of him once more, but when they rose to their feet, all it took was three shots from Shane until Davy was back on the ground unconscious.

After making sure a surprise attack wasn't possible, Shane turned his attention toward me and Summer, who was touching my bloody face. It was painful, but I managed to get to my feet. I looked at Shane and he looked back at me, but we did not say a word. Finally, we let go of everything that had happened over the past few months and gave each other a big, long hug.

Chapter 39

Eventually a few teachers found us and, after a long interrogation, punishments were given out. Shane had been suspended for the rest of the school year and I had been giving a three-day suspension for officially starting the fight. Yet, we were living it up in glory. Shane and I were finally best friends again, and to top it all off, Davy had been revoked of his graduation and was required to take summer classes before he could officially complete high school.

Summer, Shane, and I walked out of the high school and into the empty parking lot with high spirits. Life was finally perfect, except for, well, you know. Still, that didn't stop us from jamming out on the entire ride to Summer's house.

After we introduced Shane to Summer's father, we made our way to her bedroom, where Summer and I continued our ongoing game of Monopoly while Shane and I caught up.

"How are you and Camilla?" I finally asked the inevitable. I honestly didn't know what answer he had for me.

"We are doing great. Although, we decided to slow things down," he replied.

"Why didn't you hit me up?!"

"I don't know," he shrugged. "Pride, I guess."

I nodded my head and took the money Summer owed me for landing on my property, while Shane continued. "I had to retake a test with Mr. Osyphus and then I heard screaming, so naturally I followed the sound. When I saw Davy on top of you, I let everything between us go and unleashed everything I had on him."

"Well, I sure am glad you did," I rubbed my black eye. "He was beating the snot out of me."

"Yeah, dude, you should ice that," he winced. "But I got you, brother!"

Summer and I spent the next couple hours finishing our game and when she finally beat me, Shane asked what to do next.

"We could go egg Davy's house! Yeah, let's do it! We are all fast enough to get away quickly."

Summer and I glanced at each other, both with the same thought in mind. I looked back at Shane, who had caught on.

"Oh, right. I'm sorry," he said awkwardly. I didn't know how he knew though.

"It's okay," I answered for Summer. "Can we do something else?"

"What's it like? Does it hurt?" Shane ignored my question.

"Yeah."

"How long?"

"A couple more months, maybe."

"Oh, my gosh. That's terrible. I'm so sorry, Summer."

"Don't be," she pulled her hair out of her face.

"No, I actually am. I'm sorry I was such a douche to your boyfriend," he turned back to me. "He didn't need that in his life. Neither of you needed that in your life."

"All that matters now is that we are bros again."

"And bros we are! What have I missed?"

"Well," I looked over at Summer, who was scrolling through Instagram. "Summer here has taught me to live life to the fullest, something I have never been able to do."

I stared at the girl of my dreams and felt pure joy.

"Summer?" I said and she looked up at me. "Get your keys, darling. We are going to live life."

Chapter 40

Shane, the only able bodied driver between the three of us, took the driver's seat and was adjusting the seat to allow his knees more space. Summer and I sat in the backseat together as if Shane were our chauffeur. Literal nerve impulses were present in my chest as we got closer to the grocery store. We were actually going to do it; we were actually going to egg Davy's house.

As a group, we had devised a whole plan. First, we would buy our ammunition, AKA eggs, from a local grocery store. Next, Shane would drop me off about a block away from Davy's house and then position the car across the street from his house, ready to fire but also ready to escape. I would sneak into Davy's backyard from the back and begin my assault on the back of the house. As my eggs decreased, I would make my way to the front of the house, where Summer and Shane would be throwing eggs from the sunroof in her car. After we inflicted as much damage as possible, we would take off quickly and hope to not get caught.

What did we have to lose? We'd already been in trouble. But, we still fool proofed our plan flawlessly. The three of us had waited until two in the morning to leave to make sure that 1) Summer's dad had been asleep, and 2) Davy and his family had been asleep.

Even though we had greatly limited our chances of getting caught, I couldn't help but feel nervous. If you would have told me six months earlier I would be egging someone's house with Shane and Summer I simply would not have believed it at all. I never pictured myself being the type of daring or adventurous person to do something like this. Yet, here I was.

The parking lot to the grocery store was pretty much empty, except for a couple of cars that I presumed belonged to the people who were scheduled to work the graveyard night shift. Shane pulled as closely to the door as possible and waited as Summer and I went inside to get the eggs. The automatic doors opened at our presence and we were hit with a cold breeze of air from inside the store. Other than the music playing through the speakers, the store was absolutely silent. We didn't see one single worker until we had reached the eggs, where a shriveled up lady was taking inventory of sausage.

"What kind should we get?" Summer was trying to hide how tired she was. She looked really fatigued, but she had been the one most excited to do this.

"Hmmm," I examined the different kind of eggs. "Is there a specific egg best for throwing at houses?"

"Let's take a look!" she giggled.

We gave the eggs characteristics of a bomb, grading their weight, explosive ability, and many other aspects as if they weren't a food that people ate on a daily basis. After a few minutes, we decided on a couple of cartons that really had no true significance above any others.

Summer and I slowly made our way to the cash register only to find no one around. I searched the store for that lady we had seen with the sausages or a sign of any other worker, but there was no one. A few minutes passed until my patience was up and I took off for where we had last seen the lady. I had barely turned the corner when I saw her at the other end of the store, hustling my way. Hoping she wouldn't see me, I took off back for the register where Summer was waiting for me.

"She's coming."

"Okay."

The lady walked through the aisle and behind the register to check out our items.

"Sorry about that," the raspiness in her voice indicated she had smoked way too many cigarettes in her lifetime.

"No, you're fine!" I said, pretending I hadn't minded.

Without any questions or odd looks, she took the eggs and scanned them, handing them back to me.

"Four dollars and five cents, please."

I gave Summer the eggs and dug in my pocket for my wallet. After I gave the lady a five-dollar bill, she took a long time to get the remaining ninety-five cents into my hand.

Once the transaction was completed, I took the change and receipt and threw it in my pocket. But before I could look back at Summer to grab her hand, I heard the cracking of two dozen eggs on the hard tile floor. I turned around, wondering how Summer could have so easily dropped the eggs we had just spent four dollars on. But that soon became the least of my worries. Not only were the eggs laying on the ground, but so was Summer, and her whole body was rapidly shaking and twitching.

Chapter 41

When I saw Summer on the floor like that, I was certain she was dying, that right then and there her life was ending before my eyes. As terrified as the thought made me, I still clung to the small chance of saving her. I dropped to her side, repeating her name over and over again.

"Oh, my gosh!" the cashier lady yelped when she saw Summer. I had forgotten that she was even there.

"Call 9-1-1!" I yelled at her and she took off running toward the nearest phone.

"Summer? Can you hear me? Summer?" I was unsure whether or not I should touch her uncontrollably shaking body. She showed no signs of responsiveness, yet her moving eyes reminded me that she was not dead yet.

Four minutes is a very short amount of time, except for when you are waiting for the paramedics to arrive and rescue your dying girlfriend. I felt helpless sitting next to her, unable to do anything to end her suffering. The cashier lady was hovering over me, repeatedly telling me that the ambulance was on its way, but I found that more irritating than comforting.

After what seemed like hours, I could hear sirens in the distance. The sound gradually became louder until eventually I saw multiple paramedics racing in the store with a stretcher.

The paramedics wasted no time boarding Summer into the ambulance, prohibiting me from remaining by her side.

"If you are not family, you are not riding along!" the snarky paramedic told me.

Summer's dad had arrived at the grocery store right as they were carefully loading the stretcher into the car. I had expected him to come running at me furious that I had taken his daughter out so late, but he didn't even acknowledge that I was there, which made everything much worse when they slammed the doors in my face and took off toward the hospital.

Quiet tears fell from my eyes, down my face, and to the ground as I watched the ambulance drive away.

Was that it? Would that be the last time I ever saw Summer? I hadn't even gotten to have one last moment with her. I was forced away.

When the sound of the sirens dampened, I felt a hand grab my shoulder. I took a look behind me and saw Shane, who I had completely forgotten was with us, silently consoling me. I did not feel like talking and I could tell that he knew that. For ten minutes we just stood there in silence. Eventually, I fell to one knee, completely out of breath. I felt his hand come off my shoulder but I didn't bother to look up. My ears told me Shane had started the car and was driving it right up beside me.

"Come on, Uri," Shane invited me inside Summer's car. "We are going to the hospital."

I took a moment, pondering on whether I should even go, but ultimately decided there was nowhere else in the world I should be. I plopped down in the front seat and instantly became sick to my stomach as my nose was struck with a scent that reminded me so greatly of Summer.

The entire car ride to the hospital was eerily silent. I felt like talking would have made me feel better, but I did not want to feel better; I wanted to be with Summer and I wanted her to be okay. We only saw one car on the road the entire ride. I wondered under what circumstances they were driving so late at night, hoping they weren't experiencing the same pain and anxiety that I was.

Shane parked the car in a parking lot that looked similar to the one where Summer and I had met in Ann Arbor and I jogged past him through the front doors to the receptionist.

"I need to see Summer Harris, she just came--"

"Woah, woah, woah. Slow down," the lady stopped me. "Did she come through the emergency room?"

"Yes, like probably less than fifteen minutes ago."

Shane had finally caught up.

"Are you family?" she asked us.

"Kind of."

"Excuse me?" she frowned.

"I'm her boyfriend. Listen, I need to get back there. I need to see what's going on."

"I'm sorry, sir. I cannot let you back in the emergency room unless you are family."

"But..."

"There is no exceptions. You may take a seat and wait. Is there someone with her? I can have them come get you when it's time."

"Her dad," I quietly mumbled as Shane and I walked to a couple of nearby seats.

It was terrible being in the same building as Summer and not knowing how she was doing. I felt so helpless. I wanted to scream at the lady who had denied me my rights to see Summer, even though that was her job and she had to follow hospital rules.

My right leg jittered up and down while we waited for Summer's dad to come find us. Every couple of minutes I would check my phone and every time I would see the same blank screen. About an hour into waiting, Shane got up from his seat and said, "I'm going to find a vending machine. You want anything?"

"No, I'm fine," I shook my head. "Thanks."

As nice as it felt to have someone by my side during a time like this, I was glad Shane left for a few minutes. I felt obligated to talk to him when he was sitting there, and even though he was doing what any friend should do, he just felt like a burden to me right now.

When I heard someone walking toward me, I thought it might be Summer's dad, but when I realized it was just Shane, already digging into his bag of Cheez-its, I slumped back into my chair. Shane sat down next to me and chomped on his snack while I studied the receptionist for any signs of an update on Summer or when I could see her, but I got nothing out of her. Angry that she was just sitting on her phone playing a game, I walked up to her desk.

"Is there an update yet?" I bluntly asked.

"Let me check," she sighed and pushed her phone to the side.

She made a few clicks on her computer and then called someone.

"Hi, is there anyone here with Summer Harris that can come out to the front if possible? Okay, great. Thanks!"

The lady set the phone down and then turned to me, "Her father will be out soon."

"Thank you."

The term 'soon' meant only about five minutes, as Summer's dad came walking down the hall toward us at about 4 a.m. The part of me that felt scared that he might be upset with me was overpowered by my desire to find out if Summer was okay. I met him halfway, where we both stopped.

"How is she?"

He looked at me in a way that made my heart sink.

"Summer had a seizure. The doctors expect her to survive for now, but she won't live much longer, Uriah."

I had expected worse, which made finding out Summer was still living, though much closer to death, feel like heaven. I would get to hold her hand again. I would get to hear her voice again. I would be able to tell her I'm so sorry for taking her out so late at night.

"Can I see her?" I asked.

"No, not tonight," he handed me his house key. "She's sleeping right now. Go back to the house. Your friend can stay too, if you want. I'll be there in the morning and then we'll come back here and you can see her."

"I'm so sorry," I took the key. "I shouldn't have taken her out so late. I was stupid."

"Hey, don't worry about it. Summer probably would have had the seizure anyway. I'm glad she was doing as much as she could."

Was.

Out of everything he had just said, my heart shattered with that one little word.

Chapter 42

I had expected Summer's return home to be a cheerful and welcoming one, but I hit a rude awakening when I saw how terrible she looked. Looking back, I can't even describe what made her look so bad. All I can remember is that she didn't look like herself; she didn't look like Summer Harris.

Before she came home after spending three days in the hospital, I had only been able to see her twice because she had been sleeping all the time. It is depressing how much of Summer's last days were spent asleep.

The two times I did see her in the hospital were boring and uneventful. The morning after her seizure, they let me in the room to see her, but for the entire half hour I was allowed inside, she was sound asleep. The second time was at about the same time the following day and she had been somewhat conscious, but not enough that we could even talk.

That was something we did very little of in the days leading up to her death: have a conversation. Apparently it's normal for people with brain tumors to cease talking as it progresses, but it just seemed so abnormal to me that *Summer Harris* was that quiet. It sucks seeing someone trying to be happy despite the fact that they are dying, and then so suddenly take a turn for the worse. Summer and I did manage to have a couple of simple conversations, and while it had been tough, I will cherish the last memories we spent together, like this one:

It was an early morning in late June, and just like every other day since she had returned from the hospital, I woke up in a panic that she had died in her sleep. I always slept in her bed with her, and while I was terrified of waking up next to a deceased version of Summer, I knew I had to be there to comfort her. That morning, like every other, I had gotten up early to turn over to check on her. Almost every morning she had still been sleeping, but this day was different.

Rather than sleeping, Summer was wide awake, staring at the ceiling. It had freaked me out at first, but when I saw her chest moving up and down, I breathed a sigh of relief. I stroked her hair and said, "Hi, Summer."

She looked over at me with her gorgeous blue eyes and gave a half smile.

"Why are you up so early?" I asked her.

"I've," she was struggling at first, "b-been think-ing."

"About what, babe?" I continued to stroke her hair.

"About, about, when I die."

"What about it?" I had to be strong for her.

"I told-told my dad. Told him I want to be cremated. I want to be poured into the grave next to my mom. I want to be with her."

"I think that is a great idea, Summer," I smiled at her. "I love you so much, Summer Harris."

"I love you, Uriah Peterson," she said with no struggles or pauses.

Summer smiled back at me and then a couple of minutes later, she was sound asleep again. I wish I knew why that had bothered her so much because when she finally got it off her chest, she seemed free and at peace. Even though I will never know, I am glad she found whatever peace she sought in telling me that she wanted to be buried in North Carolina, right beside her mother.

Chapter 43

Summer Harris took her very last breath on July 2, 2018, three days before her eighteenth birthday. Her last and final goal had been to turn eighteen, but cancer doesn't care about anyone's goals.

She died the way the doctors had expected--in her sleep. Whoever is reading this, I hope that you never have to wake up to find a loved one lying beside you with no life inside them. I hope you never have to cling to a cold body and cry your freaking heart out. I hope you never have to walk downstairs and tell a man that his daughter will never wake up again. I hope you never have to feel the excruciating pain that I felt that morning.

Although we can never truly be ready for the death of someone so important in our lives, I had convinced myself that I was as prepared as I could be for that dreadful day. I was incredibly wrong. It is absolutely impossible to be ready for the agony of losing someone you loved so much.

I won't go through all depressing details of Summer's death day, but I will say this: it was by far the most difficult twenty-four hours I have ever experienced, and ever will experience. Crying, to me at least, hurts really badly. You can't catch your breath and you constantly feel like you are about to barf at any moment. You have to blow your nose constantly and you can't even see through the puddles of tears in your eyelids. I cried that entire day, but the pain that came from those tears couldn't even come close to what my heart was feeling.

The human heart is the basic and most obvious organ that keeps a human alive. When Summer's heart stopped beating, mine shattered into millions of pieces.

You know what I don't get? Why do people, people like Summer Harris, who was my favorite person in the whole world, have to be the ones that die so young? Why couldn't it be someone like Davy Trick, a terrible human being whose death would benefit a lot of people? I'm a firm believer in God, but this is something I will never understand. Why does He choose the best ones to die way so soon? I've done a lot of thinking about this ever since Summer died, and I've come to the conclusion that Jesus is way too complicated for the human mind and that we will never be able to fully understand. Still, it freaking sucks.

BECAUSE MAYBE SUMMER HARRIS WOULD HAVE BEEN MY WIFE. MAYBE WE WOULD HAVE LIVED HAPPILY EVER AFTER. AND HAD A BIG NICE HOUSE. WITH KIDS. AND A DOG. AND A PERFECT LIFE TOGETHER. ONE WHERE BRAIN TUMORS HAD NO PLACE.

I'm sorry. You just never really get over something like this.

Chapter 44

Even though Summer's wish was to have her ashes buried beside her mother in North Carolina, her funeral service was held in Michigan. It was at her church, which I had only visited a couple of times before she got too sick to attend anymore. Her father had already been arranging the funeral plans in his spare time before she died, so the service was held just three days after.

I woke up that morning and I wished it was all just a dream and that Summer was still alive and well, but she wasn't. This isn't a fairytale. Things never end up the way you hope for them to. The clock told me that I wasn't supposed to get up for a few more hours, but the torment told me I needed to get up and go for a jog.

My leg was actually the only part of me not in pain these days, but I still had not been cleared for intense running. It's not like it mattered anyway. I hadn't seen or spoken to my dad in weeks, and I hoped he had finally accepted that running was a sport of my past.

The cool, but bearable, morning temperatures were enough to wake me up entirely at the beginning of my run. I found it very hard to appreciate anything in life after losing what I had appreciated the most, yet I still found the sunrise in the eastern part of the sky extraordinary. The rest of sky was still dark, but soon that small sliver of brightness would illuminate everything above me.

I have been awake this early in the morning many times before, while everyone else is still sleeping and the world seems absolutely at a standstill. It is always a little eerie to me seeing a world that is constantly buzzing being absolutely still, but I had learned to be thankful for these moments.

This early-morning run gave me a brief escape; it was a rare that I was free of anyone trying to console or talk to me about Summer's passing. Many people who I didn't even know had sent me messages on Snapchat or posted on my Facebook wall telling me they were praying for or thinking about me. While it was a polite gesture, I knew dang well not one person actually said a prayer or took the time to think about me. It's just something people say to you when you experience loss in this way.

That morning I learned one very important thing: I actually did not hate running. I only hated it because my father had relentlessly pestered me, causing my love for running to fester into hate. Once I found myself jogging for my own purposes, the blindfold of hate was finally removed.

When I started seeing more cars on the roads and more sunlight in the sky, I decided it was time to retreat back to Summer's house, where I found her dad dressing in his suit way too early for the funeral. I couldn't seem to figure him out once Summer passed away. He cried for the first couple of days, but after that he seemed to mourn in a much different way. I would find him going through her old drawings from when she was a kid, or cleaning out her car. He stayed busy, which seemed like a good way to cope with the pain, but I couldn't comprehend why he would choose to stay busy by going through Summer's things.

I tell this story like I have had it so miserable, but imagine for a second what that poor guy had gone through.

Not only had he lost his wife in a boating accident, a brain tumor had also taken away his only child. He had no family anymore. Summer never even mentioned any aunts, uncles, or grandparents, and while I'm sure there had to be family somewhere out there, obviously none of them were important enough to matter.

I eventually did find out that Summer had more family than I realized; they just never came around, which explains why I had never heard of them. Summer's father shook hands and said his hellos to a few of them at the funeral, but they just gently nodded their head at me. I had no idea who they were and they had no idea who I was. I didn't see anyone that could have been her grandparents, so they must have already been deceased. Yet another thing I wished Summer was still alive to tell me about.

The funeral was tough for me in many ways, even ways I hadn't expected. I knew the hour-long service of singing songs and reminiscing on how great Summer was would hit me hard, but the fact that I felt like a stranger at my own girlfriend's funeral crushed me. Almost everyone there had somehow known Summer, yet I had never seen or heard of most of them. It made me question if I even knew Summer at all.

The only people I recognized at the funeral were kids from school. A decent amount of students that knew or knew of Summer had come to "pay their respects." The bitterness inside me thought that was bullcrap. It amazed me at how people could come to her funeral, yet when she was alive, they never said a single word to her. Why is it so easy to attend someone's funeral, but so hard to act like they exist when they are alive?

The funeral began sometime after eleven that morning with three or four common church songs. Then, a pastor talked for a long time, saying very generic things that you could say about anyone who had just died. I wished I could have gone up and told everyone what Summer was really like, but my anxiety of speaking in front of crowds got the best of me. A couple of people though, when given the chance, got up to speak about Summer and they did a better job than the pastor, but I still could have said way more from the short months that I actually knew her.

If I would have gotten up there and spoken, I would have told everyone how I had a huge crush on Summer for weeks and how the tearing of my ACL led me to meet her in the hospital parking lot. I would have explained how friendly she was to the skinny sophomore from her school, and how she was so perfect in every little thing that she did. How her nose crinkled up when she laughed. How genuinely kind she was and how she was never mean or moody to anyone. I would have explained how life never treated her fair, yet she made the most of every single second. I would have explained how brave she was, and how even though she had avoided the beach for years, she had no hesitation running into the freezing water once she found out her time was limited. She was scared, but it didn't stop her from living. If only I could have faced my fears and told everyone what Summer was *really* like. I feel like it would have done her a great justice. But like everything else in my life, I failed.

I actually held back the tears better than I imagined I would during the service, but I thought they would do a much better job than they did at telling her story. I know they really cared about Summer, but I'm too blunt to say they did a great job because I don't think they did. Summer would have been happy with it, but she was nice, and I am not.

One redeeming factor of the whole funeral service was that I had my best friend, Shane, by my side the entire time. I didn't even care that he brought Camilla, who was leaving to go back to her home in Columbia the following week. I actually thought it was really nice of her to come. I don't know what I would have done if Shane and I would not have rekindled our brotherhood because then I would have been truly alone for the first time in my life. When I lost him earlier that year, I still had Summer in my life, which made it somewhat okay. But if she had died and Shane and I had remained foes, I would have had absolutely no one. No friends, no family, and no Summer. What would I have done?

Normally everyone would relocate at a gravesite for the official burial, but since Summer wanted to be to laid at rest miles away, there was nowhere else to go after the final prayer had been spoken. I stayed in my seat for a good twenty minutes after everyone else cleared out of the sanctuary, but apparently that wasn't enough time for everyone to leave because when I exited out the large, burgundy doors I found many people socializing, eating cookies, and drinking lemonade. Steering away from anyone who might talk to me, I kept my head down until I reached Shane and Camilla, who each had a chocolate chip cookie in hand.

"How you doing, man?" Shane grabbed my shoulder.

"Better than a couple of days ago," I stared at his black dress shoes.

"That's all you can hope for."

"Uriah?" Camilla surprisingly spoke.

I looked up at her but didn't say anything.

"I lost my father when I was eleven, and from experience, I can tell you that you will never get over the pain, but each day it gets a little more better," her English had improved greatly since the last time I had talked to her, yet she still spoke with a strong Colombian accent.

"I really hope so, Camilla," I smiled. "Thank you."

I had spent the entire time I had known Camilla being jealous of her because she had taken my best friend away from me, but I had never the decency to look past my selfish ways and see her as a human being too. I would have never thought Camilla, the foreign-exchange student, would be the only one that actually said something meaningful and real to me.

I then saw a very nervous facial expression crawl onto Shane's face. Thinking about what Camilla had just said, I didn't think it would be my problem at all, but of course, it was.

"Uh, Uriah?" Shane grabbed my attention.

"Yeah?"

Instead of saying anything, Shane pointed to something behind me. Unsure of what he had seen, I turned to take a look for myself. I didn't have to look very far before I saw my father, looking very out of place, walking toward me.

Time is supposed to heal everything, even the hatred you have for someone, but seeing my father again made me remember how much I truly hated this man. Even though he looked sober and was dressed up in a suit and tie, all I felt was disgust.

"What're you doing here?"

"I came to pay my respects," he said with his hands in his pockets.

"Thank you for coming," I said sarcastically. "But you can leave now. Have a wonderful life."

"Uriah..."

"NO, YOU CAN LEAVE!" I placed my finger right on his chest. "You think I forgot the things you said about her?"

He looked from Shane and Camilla and back to me nervously, "Can we do this somewhere else. There's something I need to tell you."

"Why should I? You are a terrible excuse for a human being. If I were you, I'd be ashamed to show my face here."

"Uriah. Please," he didn't try to justify anything. I probably should have realized how serious he was.

"NO! JUST GO!" I shouted, drawing a few stares.

My father gave me the same look he usually gave me before he hit me, but with everyone around, he chose smartly. He looked very nervous, but eventually walked away and back into the church.

I tried returning back to normal after he left, but the looks I was receiving from Shane and Camilla made it impossible. On the outside I was playing it all cool, but inside I wondered how my father could possibly feel welcome to come to Summer's funeral after he told me "I just hope she dies soon so it doesn't set you back too far." My dad had crossed the thin line that he himself had created. When I saw him, I didn't see any scars or marks left from our fight, which greatly disappointed me.

Just when I began to simmer down, I saw the church doors open again. My head turned to the creaking doors and I saw not my father, but Summer's. For just attending his daughter's funeral, he had a quickness to his step. I wondered what could have made him move so fast, but I soon learned what it was as he was walking in my direction.

We were still at a funeral so he got stopped a couple of times, but when he finally made it over to me, he seemed very urgent.

"Uriah, you need to go talk to your father."

"No," I said blankly. "I never want to talk to him again."

"I promise you that you do," he looked very on edge.

"What could he possibly have to say? You should've heard some of the things..."

"Yeah, I don't care about that right now. All I know is that you need to walk into the church and speak with your father."

"I don't---"

"Uriah. Now," he said 'now' with a very assertive voice that persuaded me to finally go into the church. I would not have expected him to make me go talk to my father after knowing everything he had done to me.

I took my time getting to the front doors, occasionally looking back to see Summer's dad making sure I would follow through. I placed my hand on the brass door hand and pulled the large door open. The scent you think of when hear about a funeral was very strong in that church and as soon as I walked in, I wanted to leave.

My father was standing out in the open waiting for me. I had never seen, in all my years living with him, such an anxious look on his face. We stood facing each other silently for a short period of time until he said, "Uriah, listen."

"I'm not coming home."

"It's not about that."

"I'm not running track either!" I yelled. Hearing my echo in the empty church gave me goosebumps.

"It's not that either."

"Okay, well whatever it is, I'm not interested. I don't want you to be a part of my life again. Can you accept that?"

"I can," the two words surprised me. "But, there is something that I want to tell you. Something I have to tell you."

I crossed my arms and looked at him, ready for whatever crap he was about to tell me.

"Your mother isn't dead."

Chapter 45

"Are you kidding?" I still couldn't process what he had just told me. "But, what? How?"

"I've been keeping it from you all these years, for selfish reasons, but no, she's not dead. Not at all."

"I'm so confused. Mom's definitely dead. She was killed when I was one."

"No, she wasn't," he rubbed his eyes.

"THEN WHY DID YOU TELL ME SHE WAS?"

I did not think I could hate my father anymore that I already did, but I had underestimated that evil man.

"WHY DIDN'T YOU TELL ME?" I asked again. "BECAUSE I'VE LIVED MY WHOLE LIFE THINKING MY MOM WAS DEAD!"

"Uriah," he looked around even though the church was empty. "I know, I was selfish. I regret it more than anything else."

"Just tell me, why?" I was now shaking in anger.

"I had an affair on your mother. She found out and left me. I still love her so much."

"You know what, dad? I thought you were bad enough as it is, but you've reached a whole new level of wickedness. Okay, you had an affair, that's freaking messed up, But, you just took her away from me?"

"I know. It's my biggest regret."

"IS IT, DAD? OR ARE YOU JUST SAYING THAT?"

"OF COURSE I'M NOT JUST SAYING THAT!" he yelled right back at me. "WHY HAVE YOU NEVER SEEN ME WITH A WOMAN? WHY HAVE I NEVER GOTTEN REMARRIED? BECAUSE EVERY SINGLE DAY I REGRET THE CHOICES I MADE."

Taken back at what he had just told me, I remained silent and waited for him to speak again.

"Do you want to know why I drink so much? Why I get drunk so much? Because every sober second I have is spent thinking about your mother and how much I love her, and how greatly I screwed up. I want her more than anything in the world."

A completely different side of my father had just been unveiled to me, and yet, I could find no sympathy for him.

"Dad, I've wanted a mother so badly, but I've spent my whole life believing a lie. No, you know what? She was murdered, but not by a house intruder. She was murdered from ME through your deception and lies."

My father was now dripping with tears and though I wanted to cry too, my body had done too much of that lately.

"I hope you know this doesn't change anything," I took a few slow steps toward the door.

"I didn't expect it to. I have accepted that you don't want me as a part of your life, but I felt that you needed to know."

"I'm glad you're finally starting to get it. But not only will you never be a part of my life again, I HAVE NO FATHER. I NEVER DID."

I could see it on his face that my words had definitely hit him hard, though he deserved a much harder blow. What I said seemed like the appropriate last words that I would ever say to my father so I turned and began to walk toward the front doors of the church.

"Uriah!" my father stopped me when he realized what I was doing.

I tried to ignore his final request for my attention, but just as I opened the door a few simple words drew me back into the church.

"Don't you want to meet her?"

Throughout the shock, confusion, sadness, and anger I was experiencing in that moment, I had forgotten that my mom was actually somewhere out there and I would have the chance to meet her.

A full 180-degree turn found me facing my father again. He was holding a white envelope with the name "Lysette" written on the front.

"She lives in Tennessee. I have her town and phone number here. She gave it to me in case you ever wanted to contact her."

Without saying a single word, I stepped over to my father, snatched the envelope out of his hand, and proceeded out the door. With that, the door closed behind me, signifying the end of my relationship with my father.

The fresh, natural air outside felt like it had given me new life, and it was a relief to see that the crowd had diminished in size. I saw that Shane and Camilla were still waiting for me, but I took the opportunity to get away unseen and escaped to the back of the church where I could open the envelope.

I found a bench that was dedicated to some old man who died in the 1990s and took a seat on its white, chipped surface. My hands were still shaking from hearing the biggest news of my entire life.

My mom was not dead.

I had so many questions, like why she hadn't ever attempted to contact me? Why hadn't she taken custody of me instead of my father? I didn't know details, and I sure as heck did not plan on going back inside the church to ask my father. The lack of answers I had in regards to these questions struck a small twinge of anger inside me toward my mother. What if she was just like my dad? What if I went to Tennessee and met her only to be disappointed when I found a motherly version of my father? Still, I couldn't not open the envelope. I needed answers and I needed closure, and they were only a phone number and address away.

I jammed my pointer finger into the corner and ran it down the envelope to find a white piece of printer paper folded into thirds. I threw the envelope to the ground and unfolded the paper:

Lysette Peterson

865-001-6738

Knoxville, Tennessee

I pulled out my cell phone and proceeded to type in the numbers.

Eight. Six. Five. Zero. Zero. One. Six. Seven. Three. Eight.

The phone began to ring.

Part Four - The End

Chapter 46

So, there it is. The complete story of Summer Harris and myself, Uriah Peterson. I officially proclaimed my love for her on December 4, 2017, and she was the center of my world for the next eight months until she passed away on July 2, 2018. How greatly do I wish she could have been the center of my world for the rest of my life, but like I have always said, things in life never go the way you want them to.

I will never get over it. It's been two years since Summer died, and while the pain has gotten much better, it's something that will remain with me until I, too, take my last breath. There isn't a day that goes by that she isn't on my mind. Things in my life happen that I wish I could just pick up my phone or walk over to her house and tell her all about. I loved her, I really did, and I will always desire the need to just be with her, but that is something I will never be able to enjoy again.

But, life though doesn't pause. It moves on. Unfortunately, I can't trap myself in the past and I have to move alongside with the ongoing nature of life, and it sucks. I feel like the evolution of my life has completely removed Summer. I can't even specify details of her appearance without looking at a photograph and I can't even remember her laugh without watching a video I recorded when she was alive. Yet, I was in love with Summer Harris. Even though she is gone, she will NEVER leave my heart.

I don't know who, if anyone, will ever read this, but one thing I do know for sure is that our love story wasn't extraordinary, and it wasn't exactly this glamorous series of romantic events, but that's okay. Our love story was *our* love story. I don't care if anyone says it wasn't good enough because it was perfect to me.

Summer Harris, you were my miracle. I'm sorry that I received mine, and you didn't. If I could strip away my life's miracle and give it to you, you know I would do it in a heartbeat. You were, and you still are, my everything. I love you so much. I can't wait to see you again someday.

Uriah Peterson finished typing and closed his laptop just as the plane began descending to the ground. After a shaky landing onto the runway, the pilot announced that the plane had officially touched down in Raleigh, North Carolina.

Uriah prepared to exit the plane, but found himself stuck, waiting for a while until he was actually able to escape the warm and crowded area. Some of his fellow passengers ran up and hugged family and friends in the airport, but Uriah was expecting no one to be there waiting for him, so he made his way outside and called for an Uber. He would be back at the airport later that night.

The Uber driver needed only a few instructions before he figured out how to get to Uriah's destination. As the driver pulled out of the airport, Uriah gazed at the North Carolina landscape. From the short time he had been outside waiting for the Uber to arrive, he became aware of how warm it was in North Carolina. Michigan summers couldn't even come close to this weather. The city was full of large buildings and stadiums, along with hundreds of restaurants, stores, and NC State property. Uriah took in a small tour of the city before he found himself driving away from all of the tall buildings. Once the car hit the outskirts of the city, it didn't take long until Uriah reached his destination. The Uber driver turned right into a gated area with an archway towering over the entrance.

"You can stop here," Uriah gave the driver money and hopped out with his luggage. "Thank you."

After a long plane ride and a long car ride, he had finally made it Summer's grave. From her father's instructions, her grave would be on the northeast side of the graveyard. Passing the hundreds of monuments commemorating people's lives while rolling his luggage at his side drew a few looks from people visiting their very own deceased, but Uriah walked with a mission until he found her grave.

Summer Harris

Born: July 5, 2000

Died: July 2, 2018

"To the well-organized mind, death is but the next great adventure."

Just the sight of her grave and what was marked on it brought tears to Uriah's eyes. He hadn't known those words would be inscribed on her gravestone. He recognized the quote from the Harry Potter series, but didn't know if Summer had chosen it or if it was her father. Regardless, he thought it was absolutely perfect.

"Hi, Summer," Uriah smiled. "Oh, how I've missed you."

"It has been exactly two years since you died, and I miss you more and more with every single passing day. You gave me a reason to be important, you gave me a reason to desire life, and I'm so sorry you had to leave this Earth so soon, too young."

"Even though you are already gone, I still feel like I lose a little bit more of you every day. I'm trying to hold on, but my hands are transparent. We didn't have enough time together, but I will forever be grateful for the time we were lucky enough to have. You are the one for me, and while nothing will ever change that, my life will have to move on. I hope you understand. I'm sure you do," Uriah continued. "You were so beautiful, Summer Harris. The way your hair flowed down your body gave me the shivers each time I thought about it. Your eyes gave me instant joy whenever they looked into mine. You never made fun of anyone who didn't deserve it, and you were one of the friendliest people I ever knew. If it weren't for your outgoing personality, we would have never met and you would have never changed my life the way you did.

"Life is going okay, I guess. I just graduated from high school a couple of months ago. It's crazy to think, isn't it? I have decided on attending Michigan State this fall. I hope you're proud.

"Things have changed a lot. I haven't seen my father since your funeral. Get this, babe. My mom is still alive! My father lied to me my whole life and told me she was dead even though he had just cheated on her and felt guilty about it. I have her information and I contacted her a while back, but I thought it would be best to meet her when I came out to see you. I am actually flying over to Tennessee, where she lives, tonight and I am going to finally meet her. I wish you could too.

"I hope you'd be happy to know that Davy isn't doing too well. Apparently he had a scholarship to play Division 1 football somewhere in Ohio, but he was caught smoking pot and it was revoked! Last I heard, he was working full time at Burger King just to get by. Serves that loser, right, huh?" Uriah laughed.

"Shane and Camilla tried to date long distance once she went back to Columbia and it actually worked! He graduated after the first semester of senior year and he now lives down in Columbia with her. He's taking classes to become an English teacher. I talk to him almost every day and I am not angry at him at all for moving there. Shane really seems to have found the one in Camilla and I'm happy for him. I wouldn't expect him to do anything else.

"Your father has been here, so you probably already know how he is doing. I do see him occasionally, probably a couple times a month. It's always nice to catch up with him but, at the same time, it is really tough because I see so much of you in him," Uriah sighed.

"That's pretty much all I have, babe. It's been a very long two years. I promise I will come back and I promise it will be soon. I love you so much. Goodbye, Summer."

Uriah leaned over and kissed the part of the stone that was engraved with her name. He sat there at Summer's grave for about a half hour. A few quiet tears fell from his eyes, but in a way that was very peaceful. Although it was very tough for Uriah to leave Summer's gravesite, he eventually found the strength to take one last look, for now, and walk back toward the entrance of the graveyard.

Uriah spent the next few hours traveling via car, then plane, and then car again. Later that night, he found himself in Knoxville, Tennessee, just after the sun had set. In the span of one day, he had traveled from Michigan to North Carolina to Tennessee, and he was exhausted.

Exhaustion couldn't overcome the anxiousness he felt now, though. He had been waiting for this moment for a very long time. Uriah stood before a wooden, gray house on a very busy street. A couple of lights were on inside, which made him feel a little better when he began walking up the front porch steps.

Uriah set his luggage down and knocked on the door. Behind it, he could hear footsteps which gradually became louder until the door finally opened, revealing a kid, who looked to be about nine years old.

"Hi, is Lysette here?" Uriah was unsure of who this kid was.

"Lysette? You mean mom?"

The kid had a darker tint to his skin than Uriah, but he realized that this must be his stepbrother.

"Yes. I don't know if you know who I am, but she is supposed to be expecting me."

The boy's eyes expanded dramatically when he realized who Uriah was.

"You're my brother! Let me go get mom!"

Uriah was foreign to the idea of having a brother, which made the phrase, *"Let me go get mom,"* seem so odd.

The boy went running off and a minute later, Uriah heard deeper, more controlled footsteps coming down the hall. His palms were sopping wet and his heart rate had skyrocketed. Everything Uriah thought he knew about his mom was erased from his mind as soon as he saw the first glimpse of her.

She turned around the corner and right away, Uriah saw so much of himself in the woman standing before him. Their hair color was almost the exact same shade of brown and his nose and eyes completely mirrored hers.

"Hello, Uriah," he could see tears of joy in her eyes. "I've missed you so much."

"Hello, mother. It's nice to finally meet you."

Made in the USA
Lexington, KY
21 June 2018